AFRICAN WRITERS SERIES

Editorial Adviser: Chinua Achebe

57

BECAUSE OF WOMEN

AFRICAN WRITERS SERIES

Mbella Sonne Dipoko

BECAUSE OF WOMEN

HEINEMANN
LONDON · IBADAN · NAIROBI

D15784

Heinemann Educational Books Ltd
48 Charles Street, London W1
PMB 5205, Ibadan · POB 25080, Nairobi

MELBOURNE TORONTO AUCKLAND
HONG KONG SINGAPORE

SBN 435 90057—9
© Mbella Sonne Dipoko 1968
First published 1968
First published in African Writers Series 1969

Printed in Malta by
St Paul's Press Ltd

oṅola mwanja mu Mongo; na din
dube ma bana basu bantat' ikumbwa
mapita masu

I

Ewudu was slightly afraid of her involvement with Ekema who was taking her to visit his mother in Lysoka. She didn't know why she was afraid for she was sure she loved him. He was tall and he was strong. She didn't think he was very strong. But she loved him all the same and he had a good job. He was a clerk; and he was very proud. She liked her men to be proud.

It still wasn't a month since they met and barely a week since she began living with him and here they were on the road to Lysoka.

He could have waited until he was on leave. That would be in one and a half months' time. And then they would have made the trip. But he was impatient. He wanted her to see his mother.

Ewudu wanted to be free because she was still young and having lived with a free woman in Duala she wanted to go on playing with life, enjoying herself without being attached to any particular man. She wanted to love the most handsome and proud men and to be loved by them all.

She knew Ekema was afraid of losing her. She had made it very easy for him to have her. It therefore seemed to her that he feared it would be just as easy for her to leave him.

He loved her, profoundly, which was the reason why she despised him a bit. She thought he worried too much about her. Whenever he was like that, worrying about her, she told herself that she didn't recognize him. She always wanted the other Ekema, hard, proud and strong. And that was how he usually was until he began to doubt the future of her feelings for him.

He was a good man even though he could be very jealous.

They were now on Dibanda Hill, having left Tiko, Likomba and Mutengene behind. The deep valley was on their right and then the sprawling plain of banana plantations fringed in the distance by low clouds, the skyline and the sea.

She wondered when they would get to Lysoka. And the foolish road always went up hill, never down hill. They had been climbing and climbing and climbing; and it seemed as though that was all they would be doing — just climb until they got to his village.

Since they left the camp around three o'clock that afternoon she had been getting more and more anxious. She didn't know exactly why. Sometimes the idea of marriage came to her mind; but that was something she didn't want to think about. She didn't know whether or not she wanted him to marry her.

Crows zigzagged over the banana leaves which were very green and very beautiful.

She was a very casual young woman and she could be very insolent and vain, especially as she knew she was pretty. She was small, smoothly dark and her face looked charming and somewhat tired which lent a mellow sensual glint to her beautiful eyes.

Her breasts were small. But they were pointed and although her backside wasn't too big she had an attractive gait for she moved her waist endearingly. She was a good woman, although still young and often undecided. Sometimes she got very hysterical about the most unimportant things. But that was all right. She was a woman who loved and enjoyed life even when she was behaving most casually towards men and their desires.

She had lost both her parents. Her father had died while she was still only a little girl. And then some eight or nine years ago her mother died. How she had wept and wept!

It was exactly one week after that day in the river. Without knowing why, Ewudu often found herself thinking of that afternoon.

She had been standing knee-deep in the water when her aunt Dimene clapped her hands. It was in the dry season. The sky was blue and cloudy and sunny. And the river had been very windy.

'*Uweh*!' her aunt said. 'The growth of a human being is not difficult.' She clapped her hands again, looking at her. 'So, Ewudu,' she added, looking astonished, 'you too now have hairs?'

'Leave my daughter alone,' Ewudu's mother had said, smiling at the girl who turned her back to them because she was shy.

'Look at the lumps of her buttocks!' her aunt said and Ewudu didn't know which part of her body she could show them without her aunt having something to say; and she didn't want to swim out into the river because really she was enjoying her aunt. 'Look at her,' the woman now observed, 'soon they will be sitting on her — the misery men cause us.' Then turning to her mother, she said: 'We have brought up a girl. Let them hurry up and marry her.'

'Go away,' her mother said, 'where is she going with marriage? Leave Ewudu alone. She's still only a child.'

'Only a child!' her aunt said. 'Don't you see the tuft of hairs she already has under her?'

And, excited, Ewudu had jumped into the river and swam towards the heart of their beloved Mungo. That had been behind those banana farms and the forest, not so far away, on the great river, a few years ago.

The sound of a car disturbed the flow of her memories of that lovely afternoon and she temporarily lost sight of the past. She looked back, then in front of her and began to walk on the grass of the roadside.

She looked back again when the sound of the car grew louder,

3

and there it was, small and elegant; not very fast, but determined. A whiteman in a white short-sleeved shirt was sitting at the back. The driver was an African in uniform.

Ekema looked back to see if Ewudu was safe. The car passed, leaving behind its sound and the smell of petrol.

'Haven't you legs?' he asked.

They had come by trolley from the camp to Tiko.

'Haven't *you* legs?' she said. 'Aren't you someone who could have paid a lorry-ride for us?' she asked, admiring not the whiteman of the car which had just passed, but the driver.

In Duala she once had a lover who was a driver. He used to give her lifts in the car, when the whiteman wasn't in it, of course.

Ekema thought she was right. But it would have been too expensive. He didn't earn much money. Being a Timekeeper didn't pay much and yet one woke up very early in the morning, earlier even than the birds, to conduct roll-call. And one didn't even earn enough money to carry one through the thirty or thirty-one or the twenty-nine and sometimes twenty-eight days of kind February, the only month which knew that the earlier month-end came, the happier were the plantation's poorly-paid labourers.

Since Ewudu began living with him he had been spending twice if not thrice as much as he used to spend. He was already in debt because of her and that too worried him very much because he hated to be in debt.

And to have gone up by lorry would have meant creating an expensive precedent. They would have had to ride back to Tiko the following day by lorry. And because he couldn't afford it he felt ashamed of himself.

How he wished he had another job! How could one go on living like that, never having enough money with which to buy material happiness? And the land was so rich!

His look ran over the banana plantation and there was envy

in his eyes and in his heart. So much wealth was being taken out of the country, so much comfort. How much of it was returned whenever ships docked in the wharf in Tiko or anchored off Pfo?

Although the skyline was so cloudy he imagined he saw ships on the ocean, sailing to Europe.

He tried to imagine how life was over there, in the West of the white people. He imagined they all were rich and happy.

He was walking much more slowly now and Ewudu even more slowly because she was tired. They hadn't slept much during the night.

Tomorrow they would have to be at the Water Tank at six in the evening in order to meet the Overseer in whose trolley they had come and in which they would be travelling back to the camp.

As a boy, still at school, he had dreamt of going to the West of the white people. But now he knew that would no longer be.

They walked and walked, more or less leisurely, and Ewudu yawned from time to time, shuffling along. In some places the banana plantation was on both sides of the road; in others, a few cocoa trees and in Bolifamba, the village, and then the forest.

Every now and then a car swept past; and at Molyko a fast motorcycle which branched to the left, going maybe to Soppo or to Buea.

It was getting quite late. The air was becoming very cold and it smelled of ripe bananas.

What will I do should this girl leave me, Ekema wondered, eh, what will I do? His loin-cloth was raised in order to give his legs more freedom. The sky leaned over the banana leaves. It was a cloudy sky and the evening was getting more and more cold.

They reached Lysoka just as people were going to bed.

He knocked on his mother's door.

'Who is that?' the woman asked.

The early moon was already shining. Young people were singing in the distance.

'*Imba*,' Ekema said. 'It's me.'

He was on the low verandah which he himself had built two years ago when he had been on leave and wanted a place where he and his friends could sit in the afternoon and converse while they drank palmwine.

Ewudu was still outside, wondering whether or not she had done the right thing by coming. She thought of Duala and the city seemed even farther away than it actually was. For the first time in her life she felt she had really grown up and that soon she would be growing old. The feeling frightened her. She sighed.

The evening and the night had drawn thick clouds over the Cameroon Mountain. You saw the clouds in the moonlight.

'Ekema?'

'*E.*'

'What happened?'

'Nothing,' he said. 'I brought you a guest.'

He could smell the dry scent of the firebrands.

A pig came from the corner of the hut, grunting, followed by its young ones. They crossed the compound and disappeared under the bush which wasn't far from the hut.

Ekema's mother opened the door and he and Ewudu went in. The woman shook their hands.

'How?' she asked Ewudu, 'are you well?'

'Yes,' Ewudu replied with a smile, liking the woman.

It was so warm inside here. A lantern was on the floor and a pig was lying in the dusty ground behind the fireside, its eye half-closed, its belly turned to them.

It was a little hut. The walls and the roof were sooty. Hens

6

and a cock were on the right of the fireside, their sleep as light as their feathers.

'Sit down,' the woman said to Ewudu. And then to her son, 'But why are you arriving so late? Did you stop on the way?'

'No,' Ewudu said.

'It's because of the Overseer,' Ekema said.

Ewudu sat on a wooden stool. 'He said we should wait for him since he was going to Tiko by trolley,' she told Ekema's mother; 'but we waited and waited, *Sango* was just drinking his palmwine and conversing. Before we could leave the sun was already setting.'

Ekema sat down.

The woman who was almost as tall as her son seemed suddenly to have understood why Ekema had brought Ewudu to visit her. It was good, she thought and became very excited and happy. It is good that he should marry. And he chose well. She scratched the back of her head and turned round and went to the room.

'What shall I prepare for you?' she asked, feeling and sounding younger than her age. That was because their coming had made her very happy. 'Cocoyams?' she added, 'or plantains?'

'Cocoyams,' Ekema said, suddenly feeling very tired.

When his mother came out of the room she had a little basket of cocoyams in her hands. While she peeled them they conversed; but when she noticed that they were both a bit tired and rather sleepy, especially Ewudu, she left them alone and carried on a monologue in her thoughts.

She imagined Ewudu with Ekema's son; even a girl, she wouldn't mind, she added in her thoughts. She wanted very much to see his child. She didn't think she would mind by whom he would have the child. But now that she had seen Ewudu and had taken a liking to her, the woman wished Ewudu would be the mother of her grandson or granddaughter. How happy she would be!

7

That was why before they left the following afternoon, she called him aside.

'Now,' she told him, 'I don't want you to bring any other woman here. I like that girl. If you wish to marry, that is the girl you should marry.'

2

Ngoso thought he heard a woman grunting in the adjoining room. He emptied his coconut cup of raffia palmwine and held it to Mbongo, his younger brother.

'That wine isn't bad,' Ngoso said.

'It's good,' Mbongo said.

'But tell me,' Ngoso said, lowering his voice as his brother was filling up his cup from a calabash, 'Who's in the room?'

'Esobe,' Mbongo said, having filled up the cup and lowering the calabash.

Ngoso frowned and then took a swig of his drink.

'Whose Esobe?' he asked, sitting back.

'Esob'a Mbokaye,' Mbongo said.

'With whom?'

'With Ewudu.'

'Which Ewudu? Ewud'a Dikoto?'

'No,' Mbongo said, and gulped down some of the wine. 'Ewud'a Pondadikalo.'

'Pondadikalo la Ngila?'

Mbongo nodded, drinking. 'Yes,' he said, turning to the calabash. He lifted it to his left thigh and filled up his cup.

'Has she returned from Duala?' Ngoso asked.

'Long ago,' his brother said, lowering the calabash to the floor and then taking a long sip. He was happy; it wasn't often that he was happy. And as a habit he didn't talk much. He had lost his wife and was thinking of marrying again. But he still hadn't chosen the woman. He wasn't like his brother Ngoso who liked women too much. Mbongo was a moderate in those things. Ngoso wasn't. For him women were very important to a man's day-to-day well-being. They were a source of joy. And he wasn't very mistaken. They gave the only pleasure which mattered. Not that Ngoso thought all that. He felt it. Recently he had begun to think of marriage. Before that he hadn't been very much interested in having a wife in his house. He preferred to have women all over the place. But now he too was thinking of marriage.

'Yes,' his brother Mbongo said, 'she's back from Duala. And it looks as though a Bakweriman is going to marry her.'

'A Bakweriman?' Ngoso asked.

'That's what I heard,' Mbongo said; and then, lowering his voice, he added, 'He picked her up in Mudeka Market and she's been living with him. They've even been to Bakweriland.' He drank from his cup and then he said, 'It's this very afternoon that she returned from the market. Didn't you see her at Esadi's?'

'You know when I am with Njale,' Ngoso said, 'I can't go to Esadi's place.'

'Why not? Isn't her brother Mpanjo Esadi's lover?'

'Yes,' Ngoso said. 'And Jengu is my lover.' He drank the palmwine; and then he said, 'You know she's mad.'

'Who?'

'Njale. I haven't seen that kind of foolish jealousy before.'

9

His brother smiled.

'Will Ewudu be going back to Mudeka?' Ngoso asked. 'Is that where her man is?'

'No. They say he is a clerk in a plantation camp . . . Esobe says her man has given her two weeks to be in Mongo, his impudence!' He was speaking much louder now. 'To tell a free-born Mongo girl how long she has to stay in her native town. *Eyaye!*'

The evening was no longer far away in spite of the dazzling brightness of the sunlight. The dry season was working overtime. The sky was still blue in places and the clouds were thick and white and light, forming and then drifting slowly across the sky over the village, the forest and the river.

Compared with the light outside, Ngoso and his brother were sitting in almost half darkness for the parlour's back door was shut and its two windows overlooked the verandah, the roof of which was low.

Ewudu was actually sobbing and Ngoso could hear Esobe ordering her in a passionate undertone to keep quiet.

Suddenly Ngoso began to feel bored. It was already evening and he thought of his farm. That was where he was born and that was where he lived for his grandfather had left Mongo many years ago and had gone and settled near Missaka. And the old man had died and Ngoso's father had inherited the farm. And Ngoso had inherited it from his father.

They should have been living together on the farm, that is with his younger brother; but Mbongo preferred to live in Mongo, a village on the banks of the Mungo River where the river begins to spread out into creeks that flow into the ocean. Mbongo preferred fishing to farming which Ngoso did in addition to fishing on the river.

And Mbongo was often in the fishing ports in the south with their mangrove trees spreading as far as the horizon. The tides and the sand. Fishermen's canoes. The ribald talk and the laughter. The silence and the trawl-nets, sometimes throw-nets. The sky, low or high and the winds of the wide ocean and the sun and the rain. That was the life Mbongo preferred in spite of his calm temperament, while his elder brother remained faithful to their farm up the river. But he too loved Mongo and as their father and their grandfather had done Ngoso visited Mongo from time to time. He usually stopped on his way to or from Duala or to or from Mudeka.

He would stay in Mongo for a couple of hours; then he would return to his canoe and paddle either southwards to Mudeka or northwards to his farm. Or to Duala. Some of the visits lasted a day or two; sometimes longer as when he had gone to Mongo to attend the funeral of his brother's wife. Then he had stayed in Mongo for a week.

There were days, however, when, returning from the market, he didn't call in at Mongo. He paddled past and glanced at his ancestral beach; and if someone was on it, he called the person's name and sent a message to his people in the village, adding that he was in a hurry and so he couldn't stop.

The person who was asked to deliver the message might abuse him and ask that since when did a Mongo pass Mongo without stopping? From where had he brought that new idea? Was it because having sold plantains — they said two bunches of plantains even if there had been twenty or more — he feared they would ask him to give them some of his money? And the man would call him 'foolish Ngoso,' and say other wicked things. He would call him 'ugly-faced Ngoso,' and say even worse things even though Ngoso was in fact handsome.

To the men who abused him whenever he didn't want to call at Mongo, Ngoso replied in the same abusive vein if they were of the same age group. But if the man who had abused him was much older, Ngoso only laughed and said he had heard and he didn't return the taunts, because age was respected.

If there happened to be many people on the beach they all joined in the verbal attacks against him, something for which Mongos were noted. But it all ended in laughter.

One day someone said perhaps Ngoso was in such a hurry because he had left a woman on the farm.

'Yes,' another one said. 'It's that Pongo woman Njale. Look at his foolish face. Yes, he left Njale at home.'

'Is that why he is in such a hurry?'

'Of course.'

'That Pongo woman's thing has won over his heart. *A*-Ngoso!'

'Yes. So go, ugly-faced Ngoso. Women's Ngoso, go.'

'Look at him!'

'He is erect under his loin-cloth even more than his paddle is erect.'

'Look at his shoulders! The man! Yes, go, women's Ngoso. The son of Mbed'a Bonam, go.'

And their laughter rang out.

But there were also days when they joked less. He shouted a message to the people on the beach; perhaps a message to his brother whenever he wasn't away in the fishing port. Or maybe a message to Etondi or to Musongo in Bonamanja. Or to Bolo. Or to Endene. And from the beach came the promise:

'*O*,' the promise that the message would be delivered.

That was when he passed Mongo in the day. But he also passed it very late in the evening and sometimes in the night and when he didn't want to call and had no message to deliver he simply paddled past. Ngoso was around thirty, of medium height, and he was muscular and he had a broad forehead. Women loved him very much. That was why people called him 'women's Ngoso.'

The creaking of the bed had ceased.

Ngoso drank the palmwine; then he scratched his overgrown hair with the fingers of his left hand.

Women burst out laughing in Eyabe's compound which was behind Mbongo's. The two compounds were separated by a small bush of thorny grasses. But they were linked as all the compounds were linked with each other by one of the many footpaths which wound all over the village, linking one hearth or family to another and then to their respective beaches.

Mbongo's parlour was small. Esobe and Ewudu began to converse in low voices. Etaka, Endene's wife, called:

'*A*-Musima-o!'

'*E*!' her son answered from some two compounds away.

'*Ya e*!' Etaka called.

Ngoso beat his huge chest with the palm of his left hand.

Outside, the sunshine suddenly became more radiant, lighting up the parlour. The furniture was very simple. Two wooden chairs blackened by age. One of the chairs stood against the wall which separated the parlour from the room. The chair carried a lidless box in which Mbongo's throw-net was piled. And then there was a table. It stood against the wall on Ngoso's right. There were two *bokuka* stools, fine pieces of sculpted furniture with carvings of elephants and other animals on their sides.

Ngoso and his brother were sitting each on one of these stools. A third stool made of raffia palm pith was under the table which had lost one of its original legs. The table was as black as the chairs. A forked stick was now in the place of the fourth leg of the table. A bucket of water from the river stood on the table.

The sun was very bright outside. Ngoso felt like going; but something held him down. Maybe just curiousity. He wanted to see Ewudu's face.

And then the sun began to soften again, dimming a bit. Esobe and Ewudu became silent and the bed began to creak again. And from the river the proud voice of a canoeman rose, singing of promises.

Since it was still daylight and there were many other sounds in the afternoon, the man's voice hadn't the force it would have had had he been singing very late in the evening and in the north where the riverbanks were more thickly forested. There the forest amplified voices, making echoes of them; but here in Mongo the riverbanks were not as thickly forested and so voices on the river reverberated less. Still you could hear the man, his voice voyaging northwards; and then the creaking of the bed and legs hitting the thatched wall; for the house was thatched, walls and roof, like most of the houses in the village.

Etaka swore. Njale declared at the top of her voice that it was true. But what was true? Ngoso wondered.

While he and Mbongo had been returning from the beach a while ago, Etaka had been doing Njale's hair, weaving it into long, thin, plaits.

Now he heard Ndolo's voice. She was the wife of the man who was in the room with Ewudu. It was strange, Ngoso reflected, that the women hadn't seen Ewudu and Esobe when they were entering the house.

Etaka shouted again, saying it was god's own truth. And Ndolo affirmed that really it was true. But what was, Ngoso couldn't tell.

'What is making them to shout like that?' he asked.

'Who?' Mbongo asked.

'Those women,' Ngoso said and emptied his seventh cup of palmwine. He had arrived in Mongo almost drunk and now he was getting really drunk.

He liked the friendship between Etaka and Njale because Etaka was a good woman in the sense that she was faithful to her husband.

Ewudu began to cry again. Her voice was helpless and Esobe told her to be quiet; but she went on crying, her voice wet and hot and pained.

Outside, Njale's voice rose again. Endene's house on the

verandah of which the women were was on the other side of Mbongo's house, a little to the left and no bushes separated the two compounds. From Mbongo's door one could see the verendah of Endene's house and the people on it; that was why Ngoso couldn't understand how Esobe and Ewudu had managed to enter Mbongo's house without being seen by the women. But maybe they hadn't been outside at the time, he thought. Or they must have come in through the back door.

The parlour darkened a little more and after a while the room became silent again and it was as if Ewudu and Esobe had fallen asleep or were simply thinking, the one about his wife whose voice he was hearing from outside, the other about her lover, the Bakweriman, who had taken her to visit his mother not so long ago.

The afternoon bronzed. The winds seemed to have blown away all that had been left of the day's earlier dazzling clarity.

Ngoso felt the beginning of the future as if for the first time. Without knowing why, he found himself thinking once more of the child in Njale's womb, his child. Then he thought of Ewudu and then of the remaining lap of the voyage to his farm.

The cocoa farms. The farm houses. Men conversing under cocoa trees, their canoes down their beaches. The great birds looking slightly dreamy because of the evening.

Ngoso heard the bolt of the door of the room being drawn. The door was held open and Esobe, a smile on his face, emerged into the parlour, followed shamelessly by Ewudu.

Esobe sat down.

'*Uweh*, *a*-Ngoso,' Ewudu said. 'How are you!'

He looked at her, nodding slightly. How she had changed! How pretty she had become!

'I am well,' he said. 'And you?'

She smiled. 'I too am well,' she said and went to lean her buttocks against the table on which a bucket of water stood.

'Be careful,' Mbongo said, 'that table is lame.'

Ewudu looked behind her. It was amazing how ripe she had become. Ngoso felt something for her which made him get up without meaning to.

'Mbongo,' he said, 'I want to hurry to Musongo's place.'

'I don't think he's at home,' his brother said.

'I'll go and see,' Ngoso said and went out.

'Where are you going?' Njale asked him.

'To Bonamanja,' he said and seeing a sudden angry look on Njale's face he looked behind him and saw Ewudu coming out of Mbongo's house.

3

She caught up with him.

'Ewudu,' he said, 'so you too have begun taking the thing?'

'Wait a moment,' she said, frowning, pretending he had outraged her. '*A*-Ngoso, so you think you can talk to me any how?'

'Shut up,' he said. 'I too will have to go there.'

'Go where?'

'That's right,' he said. 'I should tell you.'

'Not a single day,' she said.

'Shut up,' he said. 'So it's only Esobe and that clerk of yours?'

'Yes,' she answered and turned away proudly, walking ahead

of him and leaving in his mind the image of her charming face.

There she was in front of him, her small shapely buttocks bobbing as she walked.

'Ewudu,' he said, 'do you know that you are provoking me?'

'Is that true?' she asked, moving her waist even more impressively, her arms completely at ease about her sides.

She knew of death and was aware of what it would mean to her body. Her breasts and her beautiful thing would become mere earth. So why not make proper use of her body while she was still alive?

That was why she was very liberal with men for she wanted them to take advantage of the fact that they had better make frequent use of what the earth would waste.

She was for men. They made her enjoy herself and she liked that very much. She had begun to feel it even when she had been quite young. Because of men she had been in a hurry to grow up, craving to participate in the pleasure she felt lay ahead; but now she was in the thick of it and she wished one could live for ever.

She was in a print dress and on her head she wore a scarf. The legs with their dimples, so beautiful, he could see under the hem of her dress as she broke into a light run down the road which had cassava farms on either side.

'Ewudu!'

She stopped, turned round and looked at him and smiled.

'What?'

'What?' he said walking towards her. 'Do you think you are still a child?'

'Am I no longer a child?'

'You?'

'Yes,' she said, waiting for him.

'Let's go,' he said when he got to her and they began to walk down the road together. 'You heard what I said.'

'That?'

'That I too will have to go there.'

'I have heard.'

'So when?'

'I don't know,' she said and as if to hide her face she turned away from him and, head down, body slightly tilted forward, she broke into a leisurely sprint, her dress dancing against her legs and thighs.

'Ewudu!'

She didn't look back and soon she turned to the right and was gone.

In front of him children were playing under an orange tree. On the other side of the road women sat in Bolo's compound.

'How?' he greeted the women. '*Lo windele*?'

'*E!*' they said; then one of them asked, '*A*-Ngoso, are you in this town?'

'Yes,' he said, passing them, an *esambu* of his large loin-cloth in his left hand.

'How is Mukenga?'

'He's well.'

'Didn't Njale come with you?'

'Why not again?' another women said. 'Does he ever go anywhere these days without her?'

Ngoso ignored her, walking very fast.

But when he got to Musongo's place his friend wasn't in. So he returned to Mbongo's house and drank two more cups of the palmwine; and then Mulobe came and the three men, Ngoso, Mbongo and Mulobe went to Kese's place where food was waiting for them.

Ngoso ate very little of the food; but when palmwine was brought out for them, he drank three cups and then he returned to Endene's compound where he ordered Njale to the beach, saying it was time for them to leave.

The sun had actually set. Hens and cocks were stalking about craning their necks at kitchen doors as if they were short-sighted. It was roosting time.

Ngoso was really drunk as he took his place in the canoe after Njale had sat down and Etaka, with Musima standing by her, was saying they should go well. Her husband Endene was away in Duala arranging for the education of their first son, Ebimbe.

'O,' Njale said, trying as much as she could to control the anger and suspicion which had welled up in her when she had seen Ewudu coming out of Mbongo's house immediately after Ngoso.

'Greet Inon i Makole for me,' a woman said.

'O,' Njale replied even though she knew she wouldn't greet Makole's wife for Njale didn't like Inon.

He began to paddle out. The night had fallen over the ocean in the south and the winds were blowing it northwards.

'A-Ngoso,' Esobe's wife said, 'will you arrive?'

'All day,' he reassured them as if he hadn't tasted a single drop of wine that afternoon and evening. 'We'll arrive, why not?'

He began to paddle with all his strength, his paddle ploughing the water noisily. Then he began to sing.

'Don't shout,' Njale cried in order to release some of her anger.

'Sing!' Esobe's wife cried from the beach. '*Muna muńenge*, sing. Man of joy, sing!'

And he sang, paddling, the canoe smoothly cutting its way through the surface of the water.

His voice was hoary. It was always like that whenever he had been drinking. But otherwise, it was rich and endearing.

He paddled and paddled and now looking back he saw the people on the beach had become small in the distance. He could barely make them out.

It was at Mulanga that Njale began to talk about Ewudu.

'A-Ngoso,' she said.

She was a big, rough woman, tall, with a full bosom and a quick temper.

'Speak,' he told her, 'your man is listening. What's it?'

'What was Ewudu doing in Mbongo's place?'

'Do I know?' he said, paddling softly.

'Do you know?' she said. 'Wasn't it adultery that kept her there?'

'Who said that?'

'Haven't I eyes?' Njale said. 'The useless thing came out of the house soaked in sweat. What other work could she have been doing there if not adultery? Eh, tell me.'

'It's I who should tell you?'

'Who else? I know Mbongo hasn't your bad habits.'

'You finally said something good about him. My bad habits.'

'Yes,' she said, 'because you think you're being intelligent, running after women all over the place. Now it's Ewudu.'

'Shut up! If you say that again I'll strike you with this paddle.'

'Come on, strike me. You're not even ashamed.' She was looking at him, having worked up her long, ugly face into a strong expression of hate. 'What are you waiting for? Strike me.'

He shook his head. 'Thank your good fortune,' he said, 'that you are carrying papa,' meaning the child in her womb.

It was almost dark now and he was paddling past late Mulobe's farm. His widow, Iyo Dimene, was washing plates on the beach. Her husband had died some ten years ago. When she heard the sound of Ngoso's paddling she straightened up, the backs of her hands on her hips. Her canoe which was small that it could carry only herself was on the beach.

'Iyo, greetings,' Ngoso said.

'Yes,' the old woman said. 'How, what news is there from Mongo?'

'No bad news,' Ngoso said, 'with exception of Dikobo who is very ill.'

'Which Dikobo?'

'Dikobo l'Ebimbe. It was Ewand'a Makan who brought the news from Duala.'

'When last did I see that girl?' old Dimene mused. 'Yes, it was at Ngambi's funeral. No, let Dikobo not do that.'

'And here?'

'Nothing special. It was your friend Makole who was here, fishing, with Mukenga. They left me my own two *biondo*.'

'Is that so?'

'Yes.'

'Good,' Ngoso said, beginning to paddle much harder, the tip of his paddle whistling through the water. 'Stay well.'

'*O*,' the widow said. 'You too go well.'

'*O*.'

4

The dusk was no longer the dusk. The evening had become the night, very dark for the stars were still not out. The river looked humble and peaceful.

Ngoso who had sweated some of the palmwine he had drunk paddled into the beach in Missaka.

Njale sighed, got up and lifted her basin with which she alighted. The basin contained the things she had bought in Mudeka. Among them were two bottles of kerosene, some salt and four cups of rice which Mwenen, Dikodu's wife, had asked her to buy for her. She had given Njale the money. And Ngoso had bought a little tobacco for his friend Dikodu who smoked a pipe and for himself he had bought some cigarettes. But he didn't smoke much. Only he liked to have cigarettes in the house so that if someone asked for one he could always give them. He was very generous.

A canoe was skirting the other bank. Ngoso could hear the voices of the canoemen, two of them, as they conversed in Duala. But their voices weren't familiar.

He too alighted. He had with him the straw bag which he used for carrying his things whenever he travelled. He put the bag down and chained the canoe to a post; then he inserted the hook of his big padlock through two links in the chain and locked it.

Njale crouched and straightening up, lifted her basin to her head. She began to walk towards the village, following a footpath.

One of the canoemen who were paddling along the other bank laughed. And the forest echoed his voice.

Ngoso picked up the travelling bag and taking his paddle he took a look at the river and his canoe and then he too began to walk up the footpath.

'*Uweh*!' old Dikodu said when they got to his compound. 'They have arrived.'

His wife Mwenen appeared in the doorway.

'I was beginning to ask whether something had happened,' she said.

'How?' Ngoso greeted, 'you saw the evening?'

'Yes,' old Dikodu replied. 'Have you arrived?'

'Yes,' Ngoso said.

'I saw Ekongo's daughter,' Mwenen went on, 'and I asked her if she hadn't seen you in the market. She said she didn't see you.' Njale put down the basin she had been carrying and Ngoso sat down on a stool. 'Then I saw Jengu's friend, Eyadi, and I asked her whether she too hadn't seen you. She said no. So I said to myself that's what had happened? Eyadi even said Jengu was wondering whether or not you went down to the market.'

'Ngoso no longer has anything to do with Jengu,' Njale said, scratching her head carefully because of the plaits which pained and itched her at the same time after the load she had been carrying on her head. She took off her headscarf. 'I've told him that the day he'd set his foot in that house he would know the kind of woman I am. Why should he have women everywhere?'

'It is in his blood,' Old Dikodu said, sounding amused. 'His father was real fire.'

'I don't want that,' Njale said, bending down.

She took the first bottle of kerosene and put it down. Mwenen went to her. Njale took the second bottle from her basin. She put it by the first bottle.

'Oh,' Mwenen said, 'how thankful I am to you.'

Ngoso drew up his stool near Old Dikodu.

'How was the market?' Mwenen asked.

'The market was good,' Njale said, straightening up.

Ngoso put his hand into his travelling bag, found the tobacco and passed it to his late father's friend who had also become his friend.

'What is it?' Dikodu whispered. 'A little tobacco?'

'Yes,' Ngoso said, smiling.

'You!' the old man said. He hadn't asked Ngoso to buy him any tobacco when Ngoso had come to their place three days ago on the eve of his departure with Njale for Mudeka Market. 'You have such bad manners!' He was fingering the tobacco caressingly, gratefully, blessing Ngoso in his thoughts. 'You went and thought of my pipe, you this son of Mbed'a Bonam! You! Well, thank you.'

23

'Oh how thankful I am to you,' his wife was saying to Njale who had bent down again and was handing her a bundle of salt.

Mwenen returned to the hut with the salt and the rice which Njale handed her after the salt. Then she came for the kerosene. She took the bottles to the hut and then when she came out again and found Njale still standing, she said:

'Let me bring you a seat.'

'Ngoso,' Njale said, turning to her man.

'We are about to go,' Ngoso said.

'Who ever told you that?' Mwenen said heatedly. 'Sit down,' she commanded. 'Food is almost ready. You'll throw a little something in the belly. You'll go there now, before Njale begins to cook. At what time will you eat? Wait and eat something,' she concluded and went into the hut, followed by Njale.

'How's the day like that?' Ngoso asked.

'How?' the old man asked, looking at the sky. He was small with rather broad ears and his head was always clean-shaven. Sometimes he got drunk and his eyes became blood-shot. 'Because of the clouds?' he added.

'Yes,' Ngoso said. 'It is as if it's going to rain.'

'I won't be surprised,' Dikodu said. 'The dry season no longer has many days left.'

'*A*-Ngoso,' Mwenen called from the hut, 'a complaint has been lodged against you.'

'What again have I done?'

'Which Ewudu did I hear that you married today in Mongo?' Ngoso burst out laughing.

'Nothing,' he said, still laughing. 'Leave Njale with her useless jealousy.'

'My useless jealousy,' Njale cried from inside the hut and soon she was in the doorway, Mwenen stepping aside for her.

'Ngoso,' the woman said, 'whose Ewudu?'

'Ewud'a Pondadikalo,' Ngoso said. 'But nothing, you hear? It is the truth. Nothing.'

'But that little girl,' Mwenen began but couldn't finish what she wanted to say.

'If you see her now,' Ngoso said.

'If you see her now,' Njale retorted scornfully.

'Is she back from Duala?'

'Since,' Njale spat.

'*A*-Ngoso,' Dikodu's wife said, 'that's very bad.'

'But he says he didn't do anything,' Old Dikodu said.

'*Na!*' his wife said, recalling those far-away days when she had had the same problems with him, 'side with him.'

'I say nothing,' Ngoso repeated.

'Then what was she doing there?'

'Njale,' he warned, 'I think that's enough. Be careful. I'll end up beating you.'

'But come and beat me,' she cried at him. 'Here I am!'

'Leave,' Mwenen said and after some serious pleading with Njale, succeeded in steering her into the hut.

Ngoso began to wonder about other times, feeling the past knew and the present couldn't tell what would be; and he wanted to know. The days would change from sunshine to rain, from clear skies to heavy clouds; and then, months later, the storms of the dawn of the year. But he wanted to know beyond all that. He wanted to know about himself.

And he was surprised at himself when he began to feel sorry for Njale because he knew she was no longer the only one who mattered more than all the others.

They later ate boiled plantains with fish and then young Mbedi arrived with his little brother Ngombe and Muyao, their young aunt and Ndenge, a cousin.

'You saw the evening?' Muyao greeted.

'*E*,' Ngoso, Dikodu, Njale and Mwenen said in a chorus

while Muyao, Ndenge and the two boys were putting down the raffia pith stools they had brought with them.

'*Di windele*,' Mwenen added. 'Your mother?'

'She saw the evening,' Mbedi said, sitting down.

'Have they come for story-telling?' Njale asked.

'Yes,' Dikodu's wife said.

Besides the stools they had brought with them, Muyao, Mbedi, Ndenge and Ngombe had brought with them *mbaka*, pieces of wood which they would beat together, rhythmically, as they sang in reply to the story-teller's solo.

'*Lo windele?*' Tamba greeted, putting down his stool. He didn't come with any *mbaka*. He would clap his hands instead.

'*E*,' several voices replied. '*Di windele.*'

'*Oa pe?*' the old man's wife asked.

'I too saw the evening,' Tamba replied, sitting down.

People continued to arrive, mostly young people, boys and girls and a few grown-up women like Muyao. They greeted, were answered and they put down their stools and sat on them, talking.

'But let us begin,' the very young Ngombe said.

'Silence!' his brother Mbedi said.

'Shall I sweep the arena?' the old man's wife asked, meaning could she open the story-telling with a short tale?

'Yes,' someone said. And the others said: 'Yes, yes.'

'Sweep the arena,' Njale said.

But the audience was still noisy. Dikodu was thinking of the story he would tell. Yes, he thought. Or should I tell the other one, he asked himself.

'When you are ready tell me,' Dikodu's wife said because the children were still making noise.

'We are ready,' Njale said and then to the noise makers: 'So you haven't heard that you should shut up?'

The noise continued. Most of them didn't like Njale who was neither kind nor hospitable. 'I say silence!' she barked.

26

'We are ready,' a young man said.

'Now silence,' a girl said.

'I say silence!' Njale cried. 'Or are you all drunk.'

'If it is so,' the old woman said, 'your father Dikodu won't tell you a story tonight.'

'No!' the children protested. 'No!'

'No,' a boy added.

'No,' another boy said.

'Pa Dikodu you are going to tell us a story,' a girl said, playfully speaking like a very small girl.

But instead of becoming silent they continued to whisper noisily.

'It looks as though you don't want to listen to stories tonight,' Mwenen said.

'*A*-Ndenge, *diba*,' Muyao cried.

'It's not me,' Ndenge protested.

'*A*-Tamba!' Muyao remonstrated. 'Eyadi!'

Muyao then suggested that there should be *musisingi*. Everybody agreed with her.

'I am the elephant's heel,' a youngman said.

'I am the tiger's claw,' another young man said.

A girl said: 'I am the bee's sting.'

'You must be honey,' a rascally young man said. 'I am the lion's claw.'

'How?' the girl said. 'What is honey supposed to do?'

'Nothing,' the rascally boy said. 'It's supposed to be sweet, that's all.'

'*Na so*!' Muyao scolded the boy. 'You have started; and then turning towards the girl she said: 'Be the bee's sting.'

'No,' the girl said. 'Let him not kill me. I'll choose something else.'

'I am the turtle's slap.'

'I am the antelope's horn.'

27

'Pa Dikodu,' a very young girl asked the story-teller, 'what will you be?'

'The storm.'

'The storm?' the girl asked.

'And you Ngoso?' an almost ripe girl asked.

'The whip,' Ngoso said.

'O o o-ho!' some of the children said in mock dread.' The whip?'

'Yes,' Ngoso said, 'so hold your tongues.'

So they continued to choose the manner in which they would punish anyone who made the least noise while a story was being told. He or she would be clawed by the two young men who had respectively chosen to be the tiger's claw and the lion's claw. Almost simultaneously the noise-maker would be butted as an antelope would butt, stung by the bee (a pinch more or less painful depending on the boy), bitten by the aunt (another pinch), whipped by the whip (probably a real stroke, depending on Ngoso's mood), trampled upon by the elephant heel (a foot placed on the noise-maker's head), slapped, blown down by the storm (a token push) and so on.

Two people came down the footpath which ran along Dikodu's compound. They were talking and walking very fast, their loin-cloths raised a bit because of the grasses of the roadside.

'How, you saw the evening? one of them greeted.

'E!' Dikodu, Mwenen, Ngoso, Njale, Ngombe, Mbedi, Muyao, Tamba, and the rest of the audience answered. And the two men went on their way.

'*Musisinge e!*' a youngman cried, his voice urgent.

'*Mboke e!*' the others, including Dikodu and his wife, replied.

'*O kidi e!*' the young man added.

'*Womi e!*' they all replied and silence settled over the compound.

'*Uweh!*' said Mwenen who had the right to speak because she was going to tell a story. 'I don't know which story to tell. I have two stories. One is long. The other is short. Which one do you prefer?'

No one spoke. It was as if they weren't hearing her. But they were listening, waiting and all their eyes were turned towards her as presently she began to tell them the story of a fisherman who had many wives.

She told the story with feeling and even Ngoso was moved. The man loved one of the women more than the others. Whenever he returned from the sea he would give the best of his catch to the woman he preferred while he gave the other women little, bone-ridden fishes.

When the women discovered the extent of the man's partiality, they got hold of the woman he loved best and tied her to an ant-infested tree while he was at sea, fishing. The ants bit and bit the woman until she felt she was going to die. The sky was touched by the first light of the day. She began to sing, reporting to her husband what the other women had done to her.

'Listen,' the fisherman told his helmsman, 'that's my name that is being called. Can you hear it?'

The voice was coming from far away.

'It's your wife,' the helmsman said, recognizing the voice.

The woman was saying that ants were eating away her eyes.

'Yes,' the fisherman said. 'I don't know what they have done to her.'

The sea was losing its phosphorescence and the first birds had appeared on the half-dark shore.

'Let's paddle home,' he said to the helmsman.

They paddled and paddled while the voice of his dear wife became thinner and thinner until it was barely audible in the noises of the morning.

The sky was cloudy and the breeze cold and moist.

From the way Mwenen told the story you thought she was

29

seeing it all before her eyes, that very moment, seeing the sea and the fisherman and his helmsman in their canoe and hearing the woman's sad voice.

There was much sighing in the audience when the story ended.

Muyao had heard it before, in Jebale. Some two or three children had fallen asleep, leaning their heads on the lap of an elder sister, cousin or young aunt.

The audience relaxed, chatting, for now that the story had come to an end they could talk. Some laughed, recovering from the feeling with which the dramatic events narrated by the woman had affected them.

'Pa Dikodu,' a little boy said, 'we are waiting for you.'

The old man cleared his throat and then sighed. Someone called for silence.

'*Myango*!' Dikodu said.

'*Mbenge*,' the audience replied.

He too talked of love, developing his story from painful events, all sorts of difficulties against which the lovers had to struggle, difficulties created by the wicked and envious hearts of the world, through the relentless resolve of the lovers and finally to their victory which was to be brief for their plans were later defeated in tears and in death.

A long, sad story, longer and sadder than the one his wife had told, even though the theme was the same. And the forest was silent as if it too was listening.

The old man taught them a chorus which they sang in reply to his solo and he joined them in singing the chorus and they beat their *mbaka*, some clapping their hands.

A long, sad story of love and voyages, of long journeys through the forest, of people losing their way and their voices. A stormy forest in the rainy season. Flooded rivers and lovers. A low, cloudy sky, wet and without stars. No moon. And most of the days were without the sun. A boy in the forest.

30

When the story ended, Njale carried her basin and Ngoso took his paddle and bag and having wished Dikodu and his wife goodnight, telling them to sleep well and they having wished them the same, they walked away from his compound, following the footpath that led to the river.

Mbedi, his young aunt Muyao, Ngombe, Ndenge and a boy and a girl who had come from Mwanda walked ahead of them in a single file.

5

It was a dazzling morning. Ngoso sat at the helm of his canoe, leant forward and began to bail out the water which had gathered in the canoe during the night. It had a stubborn leakage problem. He had stopped all the cracks with rags and *ndobo*; still the water found its way into the canoe.

He heard the sound of a launch from the south. The last dew was rising from the grasses of the riverbanks — a thin vapour, thinner than a clean maze of spider's web, almost as intangible as air — towards the white clouds which the wind was spreading against the sky.

He bailed the water with a *mboso*, using his right hand while his left hand held his paddle in the river. The canoe was drifting, carried by the current. Monkeys were on the branches which hung over the riverbank.

When he finished bailing out the water he dropped the mboso in the canoe and sitting up, he began to paddle upstream. He was going to Makole ma Dikuta's place.

A heron. Strange that the previous evening it had seemed as though the first rain of the season was going to fall during the night.

Trees and green grass stalks on the banks. Some of the elephant grasses grew out of the water.

An eagle made a short flight on the left bank.

Ngoso's spirits were very high that morning. He felt happy and healthy. It was as if he had never known sadness; as if he hadn't mourned his father and his mother. Their graves were at the south end of his farm. An uncle had also been buried there. But just now he wasn't thinking of death. He was thinking of the child in Njale's womb. If it turned out to be a boy, he would name it after his father; and if a girl, after his mother. But he wanted it to be a boy.

'Mbed'a Ngoso,' he thought hopefully.

His father had had two wives. Their mother was the second wife whom their father had married because his first wife hadn't been able to give him any children; and since he wanted to found a village on the farm, he had to take another woman. She became pregnant and Ngoso was born and two years later his brother Mbongo.

As Ngoso grew up he came to love his step-mother's youngest sister, Longele, very much. Whenever she took him and Mbongo to Bojongo, Ngoso was very excited. He became attached to the game of the tides on the beach, to the funny behaviour of the scuttling mudskippers under the dangling roots of the mangrove trees. The ebbing and flowing of the tide down there in the south. Up here, where he had his farm, the tide was imperceptible unless one was very observant, or unless one imagined it. Bojongo of years ago!

And it was also there that he and Mbongo had gone to school and had learnt to read and write Duala for three years. And Longele had helped them a lot with their school work, especially as she herself enjoyed reading from *Nimele Bolo*.

But that was the past. He was a big man now.

He met his friend and his pregnant wife Inon sitting under the cocoa trees just above their beach. Inon's belly was so large that she could no longer wear most of her dresses; not that she had many. This morning she was wearing a blouse and a loincloth which she tied as high as her armpits.

'How?' he greeted them. 'Did you come out?'

'Yes,' they replied, 'we came out. And you over there?'

'We came out,' Ngoso said.

'Ugly-faced Njale?' his friend Makole asked.

He was mending a throw-net, his wife sitting about a yard or so away from him. She was peeling beans with the nail of her right thumb.

'Shut up,' Ngoso said. 'My goddess of a woman!'

Inon burst out laughing; for to her Njale's face was ugly. Or so many people thought. But there were others who thought she was pretty. And her stout body was definitely shapely.

'What did he say?' Makole asked even though he had heard Ngoso.

'He said his goddess of a woman,' Inon said, 'Please *a*-Ngoso, don't kill people with laughter.'

'But of course,' Makole said.

He was compactly built and was more handsome than Ngoso. He was very rascally and his wife didn't respect him as much as she respected Ngoso.

They conversed for a long time and then Ngoso said they should come to his place.

'To do what?' Inon asked.

'Njale brought some very good things from the market,'

Ngoso said, 'Come and eat them. It's a long time since you came to my place.'

'Was it she who asked you to call us?' asked Inon.

'Why?' Ngoso said.

'Ngoso, your woman,' Makole's wife said, shaking her head, an expression of disgust on her face. 'I don't know why she hates me.'

'Who told you that she hates you?'

'A,' the woman said. 'Don't you see the way she looks at me? Whether she thinks I want to take you from her I don't know.'

'Shut up,' her husband said, at once joking and serious. 'Take who from whom?' He looked round at Ngoso. 'Try. You'll shout my name from your grave.'

Ngoso laughed. Makole and his wife smiled.

The two men had been friends since childhood when their respective farms had been run by their parents. Like Ngoso's father, Makole's father was now dead. But his mother was living, although precariously. She was in hospital in Duala. Inon's younger sister was there, taking care of the old woman.

Although Makole could talk like a violent man, he really wasn't violent. Ngoso was and sometimes he wished he wasn't so violent.

'Njale doesn't hate you,' he said to Inon.

'Maybe,' the woman said with a resigned air. 'But she doesn't like people at all. Whenever people are in the house she twists her face like I don't know what.'

'And what a face,' her husband said.

'Leave my woman alone,' Ngoso said.

'But brother,' Makole said, looking at Ngoso and Inon over his shoulder. 'Is she a fish that you'll say Makole has caught in the meshes of his net?'

'Njale is my eye,' Ngoso said, his voice full of affection.

34

'*Aye!*' Inon said, making faces. 'Don't pluck my heart. Njale is your eye?'

'All day,' Ngoso intoned. 'Mbed'a Ngoso is in her.'

'Is she pregnant?' Makole's wife asked, looking at him.

'A long time ago,' he said proudly.

She was very happy for him because he was going to be a father. It didn't matter that he would be having the child by Njale whom she didn't like very much.

'I said it again,' she said. 'I thought I saw it on her cheeks. Whether it is that pregnancy which makes her to be like that . . . "

'Shut up!' her husband said. 'Like how?'

'The way she is always twisting her face when people come to their place.'

'I say shut up,' her husband repeated. 'You've been carrying yours for all these months, is that how you are too?'

'What do you want me to say?'

'Njale is not kind, that's all. She alone, a bitter face with a wicked heart.'

'Gently,' Ngoso said. 'You think you can compare my woman with this useless thing sitting here?'

'Shut up,' Makole said. 'Inon, listen to that.' He shook his head. 'Ngoso, Njale? To compare her with my star?'

'Where's the star?' Ngoso asked even though he knew as everybody else that Inon was extremely pretty. 'This useless thing?' Inon looked at him; their eyes met. She smiled and turned her eyes to the beans she was peeling. 'She laughs,' Ngoso said.

They went on conversing until the launch appeared, a small launch towing two large lighters. Mbam, mbam, mbam, mbam, mbam, and waves spread out to the riverbanks.

Clothes were spread out to dry on one of the lighters. Mbam, mbam, mbam, mbam . . . Smoke and the smell of gas oil.

And then Ngoso said he was going.

'We are waiting for you,' he said. 'Don't delay too long.'

'O,' Inon said.

'And don't forget a little palmwine,' Makole called after him.

'O,' Ngoso said, stepping into his canoe.

6

But when he got home and told Njale that Makole and Inon would be coming and so she should prepare some food, she said she wasn't going to cook for them.

At first he wouldn't believe she was being serious; but when he saw the frown on her face he knew she meant it. He decided to treat her mood lightly.

He went into the room and took some money from the sum he had brought from the market where he had sold plantains. He would also pay the palmwine tapper the sum he owed him, he thought.

'I am going to Missaka to buy some palmwine,' he said when he returned to the parlour. 'You heard what I said.'

'If you want them to eat when they come you'll have to do the cooking yourself,' she said, sitting down. 'I'm not going to burn my fingers and smoke my eyes because of your lover.'

'Who again is my lover?'

Njale sprang up.

'You think I don't know that you sleep with Inon? And since Makole is so stupid he can't see what is happening right under his nose! He'll bring his large mouth —' Makole's mouth wasn't large — 'to come and drink. Go and buy him palmwine. That's what you bribe him with.'

'You aren't well,' Ngoso said because what Njale was saying was a lie. He had never desired his friend's wife.

'I'm not well? Are you going to deny that you sleep with Inon?'

Bwai!

The slap had struck Njale's face before he realized what he had done.

She stared at him. Big, immobile, she stood there looking as though it wasn't she who had been slapped.

Ngoso's anger increased. Did she want him to kill her with his hands? She wasn't even crying as if the slap had been the feel of a leaf dropping against her cheek. He knew it had been quite a hard slap.

He looked back at her and then he shook his head. His temper began to cool down. Thank your good fortune that you are pregnant, he thought. I would have maimed you with my hands. Thank your good fortune. He turned towards the door.

'Thank your good fortune,' he repeated aloud, and went out.

The sun was intense. It was around noon. The sky was immense and very high and blue. The branches of the forest behind his farm was stirring in the wind. He could hear grass-hoppers complaining, tickled by the heat.

That I sleep with Inon, he thought. No; that talk musn't be heard.

The river was below the hill on which his hut stood in the heart of his farm. The river was iridescent in the sun, green here, sparkling wavelets there, and dark under the shade of the trees on the opposite bank.

37

Down the beach his moored canoe was being pushed by the wind, northwards and then the current would swing it back, southwards. He had left his paddle in it, knowing he won't be long in the hut.

'If you think I'll cook that food,' he heard Njale's voice ring out of the hut, 'then you are fooling yourself.'

'What do you say?' he asked.

'You heard me,' she spat from the doorway and then she withdrew into the hut.

Ngoso's anger rose and unable to control it, he strode back to the hut, wrinkles on his forehead. Maybe she was going mad, he thought furiously and felt his powerful arms grow light, ready to punish her for all the provocation her jealousy and imagination were mounting against his patience with her. It was terrible that she was trying him thus. Maybe she wants something from me, he thought. Her foolishness! I'll teach her.

'What do you say?' he asked, stepping into the hut.

Njale didn't reply. She just stood there, tall, big-breasted, her eyes big, her nose prominent, her lips full.

'I say what do you say?'

'I say if you think I'm going to cook for that harlot — ' Inon wasn't a harlot; she wasn't even wayward — 'then you are fooling yourself,' Njale cried into his face, her body tense, all her life ready for his temper; and it reacted.

Bwai!

It was a very hard slap. 'My teeth!' she cried, bending forward, her face in her hands.

'Your teeth!' he cried back and slapped her again. 'Open that useless mouth again. Say you won't cook this afternoon. I say repeat what you said!' And bwai! he slapped her again.

'*Ayo!*' she wailed, staggering backwards until her buttocks butted the wall behind her. '*Ayo!* Ngoso will kill me today. *Ayo!* Ngoso kill me today. Kill me today. It's today that you

38

are going to kill me.' Bwai! another slap. '*A*-Ngoso, kill me today,' she wept. '*Ayo! Ayo!* Kill me today. *A*-Ngoso, kill your child as well. Ngoso, kill your child. *Ayo!*'

Bwai, bwai! 'Shut up. I'll scatter your useless mouth. Kill your child, kill your child — '

'Yes, kill your child as well,' she cried.

He slapped her again. 'Kill your child, kill your child,' he fumed. 'Aren't you ashamed? The child is in your womb —' bwai! — 'and not in your foolish mouth!' Bwai, bwai! 'Your foolishness.'

'*Ayo!* You are going to kill me today,' she wept, her face wet with tears, blood running down the corners of her battered mouth. '*Ayo!*'

That's enough, he thought. He turned and began to make for the door. But before he had taken two steps she charged at him from behind and wrapping her long arms round him she tried to lift him from the ground in order to throw him down.

'Your lie!' he exclaimed, planting himself firmly on the ground and, swinging round, took her right forearm in his left hand. It was a blistering hold. She felt the pain right down her hips, down the muscles of her thighs. It made her jut her buttocks backwards. Passing his right arm over her head, he put it against her neck and pressed it, hard, pushing her neck away from him.

Her arms weakened about him. She jogged backwards, like a drunkard hit on the forehead; and then, falling against the wall, she dropped on the ground and he was at her, beating her as he had never beaten a woman before.

'*Ayo, ayo, ayo!*' she wailed, wallowing on the ground. '*Bíno ya e!*' And from the river came the wind-borne voice of a canoe-man singing of hope, paddling with the current and the wind; and Njale wept, crying: '*Ayo!*'

As he was standing over her, he was already feeling sorry

39

for her. It was strange that now he didn't want to think of the fact that she was pregnant.

'Now you know what you must do,' he said when she had stopped to cry and was only sniffing.

She didn't say anything and he went out.

He was soon in his canoe, paddling to Missaka.

A heron overtook him. The bird alighted on an island of sand which was strewn with dry branches and beetle-eaten logs.

Because of the dry season the river wasn't very deep; and on the left bank along which he was paddling it was very shallow and he could see the brown sand of the riverbed.

Small birds were dancing on the island of sand, beautiful birds on the sand just for the pleasure of it, it seemed, while larger birds – Ngoso could count three: the heron and two other birds – paced the shore of the little island, necks out, beaks ready to peck at fry and weeds and whatever other thing that might excite their curiousity or appetite. A tuft of grass was growing on one of the larger logs the river had lodged on the island.

The heron pecked at something in the water.

On a log on the other bank a crocodile lay basking in the sun, his long mouth held wide open, a natural fly trap.

The afternoon glowed, and Ngoso paddled softly while in his imagination he seemed always to be hearing Njale's voice.

7

'Now is it right that you should be beating Njale like that?'
Muyao asked him as he was paddling into the beach.

'Who told you?'

'Atangana,' the girl said, 'that's him going.'

Yes, the Ewondoman's canoe was on the beach with two
others.

'*A*-Muyao,' Ngoso said, 'Njale has too many bad habits.
I'm tired of her.'

'Is that why you should beat her as if she's an animal?'

'But who said I beat her?'

'I say Atangana did,' said the girl.

'I simply wiped a little dust from her cheeks with the back
of my hand,' he said.

'A little dust,' the girl said, 'you aren't even ashamed. Get
up and go to the village. Don't you see that I am waiting for
you? I want to bathe.'

Ngoso met old Dikodu and two friends drinking palmwine
under the shade of a *sao* tree. The old man must have been
returning from the river. He was very clean and he wore a fine
loin-cloth. He had rubbed himself with palm kernel oil and his
clean-shaven head shone.

'Sit down,' he said, handing Ngoso a cup which he filled up
for him.

Ngoso drank and licked his lips thoughtfully.

'That's Malende,' he said.

'Yes,' the story-teller said.

'I said it again,' Ngoso said. 'He taps very good wine.'

'Malende knows a lot,' one of the old man's friends said.

'I don't know if he still has a calabash left,' Ngoso said.

'I think he has,' Dikodu said.

Ngoso emptied his cup.

'Last night we were here until the dawn.'

'Listening to stories?' one of Dikodu's friends asked.

'Yes,' Ngoso said.

'Dikodu with his lies,' the story-teller's friend said. 'I don't know how some people have so much breath.' He looked at Dikodu. 'You sit through a whole night, telling nothing but lies.'

'But you are saying,' the other man said, 'as long as there are people who want to hear him.'

'But a-Ngoso,' said Dikodu's friend, 'you also can sit through a whole night listening to his lies!'

'It was because of Njale,' Ngoso said, 'she loves to hear stories.'

'How did she come out?' Dikodu asked.

'She came out well,' Ngoso said.

Dikodu's wife was away in one of her farms.

'Shall I add?' Dikodu asked.

'No,' Ngoso said, putting the cup down. 'I'm in a hurry.'

He got up and followed the footpath to Malende's compound. The footpath ran through cassava farms.

The palmwine tapper and Atangana were on the verandah, drinking palmwine. Firewood was being split in the back yard.

Malende was in a small loin-cloth. His torso was bare. He had a large, hairy chest. Ngoso's wasn't as large and not as hairy. Atangana was in a khaki pair of shorts and a calico shirt.

'Greetings,' Ngoso said.

'E,' Malende replied. 'How, you came to visit us?'

'Yes,' Ngoso said. 'Have you a calabash left?'

'I don't know,' Malende said.' I'll have to look. But won't you sit down?'

'Why not again?' Ngoso said, sitting down.

'How's Njale?' the palmwine tapper asked.

'She's well.'

'She's well,'the palmwine tapper said, 'with all the beating you gave her.' He drank more palmwine, and then he said, 'That's what Atangana has been telling me. He was on the river while you were beating her. But you know him. He never stops a fight.'

'But who was fighting?' Ngoso asked. 'I Ngos'a Mbedi, to fight with a woman? Not a single day. I beat her, that's all.'

'You beat her,' the palmwine tapper said.

'Njale is too headstrong, a-Malende.'

'How many times will they have to tell you that that is not how to handle a woman?'

'How is a woman handled?' Atangana asked scornfully.

'How is a woman handled,' the palmwine tapper mimicked. 'Aren't you like him? They tell you not to beat women anymore, you won't listen. And then that Njale with that child she has in her belly.'

'Who said she has a child in her belly?' Ngoso asked.

'What does the way she looks mean? See how smooth she is.'

'She isn't pregnant,' Ngoso said.

'Woman,' the palmwine tapper called his wife.

'How, a-Ngoso,' she said when she appeared.

'*Nyango*,' Ngoso said.

'Visiting us?'

'Yes.'

'Listen to him,' the woman's husband said. 'He says Njale isn't pregnant.'

The woman frowned questioningly at Ngoso.

'Njale is pregnant,' she said emphatically. 'Hasn't she told you?' Ngoso lowered his look, scratching the corner of his head.

'He knows!' the woman laughed, looking at Ngoso. 'He was only joking. The man!'

She had begun to lose some of her teeth. But her little bony face still had a certain charm of its own.

'Be careful the way you handle her now,' she advised him, 'because she's no longer empty.'

'Don't beat her again,' the palmwine tapper added.

'I have heard,' Ngoso said.

'Don't treat her lightly,' said the woman. 'You know what she's carrying in her belly is your late mother's dream. *Uweh!* If Endal'a Bola had been alive now, what joy it would have caused her!' She sighed, seeing Ngoso's mother in her memory. 'Death, only you do know.' She sighed again and turned towards her husband. '*A*-Malende, what will you like to eat? Cassava or cocoyams?'

The palmwine tapper looked at his friend.

'Atangana, what?' he asked. 'Cassava or cocoyams?'

'With what?' The Ewondoman asked, looking at Malende's woman.

'With a little roast fish,' the woman said.

'Then cassava,' Atangana said.

The woman went back into the house.

Malende took a cup and leaning forward held it to Ngoso.

A cock beat his wings on the other end of the verandah and crew.

'First take your money,' Ngoso said, rising from his seat and putting his hand in his pocket.

He brought out some cash in the palm of his hand.

A cock crew in the distance, some three compounds away. The sun was getting even more intense.

Ngoso counted the money from his right palm to the palm of his left hand; the amount he owed the tapper and the cost of a calabash of palmwine. He put the balance into his pocket and returning the money in his right hand he handed it to the palm-wine tapper.

'Money?' Malende said, putting down his cup. 'What will I do with it?'

The cock at the end of the verandah beat his wings again and crew. Near him were two hens bathing in the dust they had made since the beginning of the dry season.

'Don't you want it?' Ngoso asked.

'No,' the tapper said, looking at the money in the palm of his hand. 'The whole of my house is full of money — '

'If it is so,' Ngoso said, sitting down, 'then give it back to me.' He held out his hand to him. 'Give it back to me.'

'No,' the older man said, as if reluctantly. 'Since you insist that I take it, I'll take it.'

'No, give it to me since you don't want it.'

'I'll take it,' the tapper said, 'to please you.'

They laughed and the tapper put the money by the calabash of palmwine which was the joy of that afternoon.

'You,' Ngoso said, taking his cup, 'to refuse money?' He shook his head. 'Come on, let's see if the useless wine is drinkable.'

The tapper looked at him; then at Atangana who was smiling; then at Ngoso again. Malende smiled, shaking his head as he lifted the calabash and filled up Ngoso's cup.

'No wonder Njale can't stand you,' he said, putting down the calabash.

'She'll stand me,' Ngoso said.

'Only don't beat her again.'

'I say I have heard,' Ngoso said, tasting the wine. 'I just played with her cheek.'

'Played with her cheek?'

'Yes,' Ngoso said and drank more of the palmwine.

'That's right,' Atangana said, emptying his cup. 'He just

45

played with her cheek,' he said, and wiped his mouth with the back of his hand; he smiled. 'Fill up my *mponde*.'

The tapper filled it and then he filled his own.

'*A*-Malende.' Ngoso said, 'that wine is bad.'

'Is that so?'

Ngoso nodded, drinking. When he had emptied the cup and because in spite of what he had said he really liked the wine which was very strong, he said:

'What bad wine!'

'Go and vomit it,' Malende said.

'Yes,' Ngoso said. 'On my way back.'

'On your way back.'

'Yes ... Fill up.'

'Fill up what?'

'Put just a drop.'

'A drop of what?'

'Of that useless wine.'

'But I thought you said it was very bad?'

'I know,' Ngoso said. 'That is why I am asking for just a drop.'

Malende shook his head. He began to fill up Ngoso's cup.

'Mongo,' he said.

'Enough,' Ngoso said when the cup was half full. But he was still holding it to Malende.

The tapper put a little more, and looked at the young man.

'I say enough,' Ngoso said, still he held the cup to Malende who shook his head again and poured a little more of the wine into the cup.

'Why are you filling up the cup?' Ngoso asked. 'I told you that was enough.'

'Your lie,' Malende said.

They laughed and drank and talked and drank.

A cassava farm, the palmwine tapper's, stretched from the

other end of the compound to the edge of the forest in which dry branches were snapping. They could hear them. Ngoso and Atangana and Malende could also hear the afternoon heat splitting open the dry husks of wild fruits, the wind dispersing the pods.

And then they fell silent. Ngoso thought of Njale. The story of the fisherman had seemed to encourage her in her wilfulness. She had looked pleased about the fate of the woman the fisherman had preferred. She was dead by the time her husband arrived back in the village.

Ngoso recalled how the second story had changed Njale's feelings. She looked afraid and had wiped her eyes several times.

He wondered what thoughts had found their way into her heart? He would have to hurry back to the farm and talk to her about her doubts. He would play with her in order to reassure her.

'I say that is no sunshine!' Atangana exclaimed, gaping at the glaring afternoon.

'But that is rain,' the tapper said. He was the oldest of the three men. 'The rainy season has delayed this year.'

'When it comes,' Ngoso said, 'it looks as though it will be something else.'

'It might not be heavy,' the tapper said. 'Look at two years ago. That was how it delayed. People began to say it will be terrible. But when it came there were virtually no floods.'

'That is true,' Ngoso agreed with him, recalling how scanty the harvests that followed had been.

He emptied his cup, feeling an upsurge of pity for Njale.

'Bring my calabash,' he said, putting the cup down.

Yes, he would talk to her, he reflected. He hoped he would succeed in convincing her about Ewudu and Inon; and he felt his manhood asserting itself, stretching out his desire towards Njale.

The tapper got up and went into the house.

A touch of freshness sneaked into the afternoon. A light cloud had moved against the face of the sun, casting a brief shadow over the village.

The cloud passed, blown by a capricious wind.

Malende came out with a calabash of palmwine which he gave to Ngoso.

'*A-nyangá*,' Ngoso called the tapper's wife, 'I have gone.'

'No,' the woman said from the backyard where her kitchen was. 'Sit down and eat a piece of cassava.'

'No, thank you,' Ngoso said. 'Makole and his wife are coming to my place. Perhaps they are already there. I'm hurrying to go and meet them.'

'*Na?*' the woman asked.

'Yes,' Ngoso replied. '*A*-Malende, thanks.'

'*E*,' the tapper said, 'only be careful with my calabash.'

'Atangana, I have gone.'

'*O*,' said the Ewondoman.

'So greet Njale for me,' Malende's wife said when she came to the verandah.

'*O*,' Ngoso said, turning towards the footpath which led to Dikodu's compound and from there to the riverside.

'How?' the story-teller said when he saw him passing, 'are you on your way back?'

'Yes,' Ngoso said.

8

When he got to his hut he put down the calabash of palmwine in the parlour and went into his sleeping room where he leaned his wet paddle against the wall behind the door.

He returned to the parlour. The back door was open; but he could hear no sound from the kitchen.

'*A*-Njale,' he called in a very friendly voice.

He had no answer. So he went to the kitchen. She wasn't there and there was no fire in the fireside.

Where was she?

He went under the cocoa trees which were behind his hut. Dry branches broke under his feet as he walked and dead leaves rustled noisily, almost painfully. He got to the footpath which ran along the river and walked along it until he got to the little burial ground which marked as it were the end of his farm on the southern side. He threw a nervous glance at the grasses which were growing on the depressing mounds of earth, and then he turned his look towards the river.

He turned round and walked back to the hut, a frown on his face. He went into the room. That was when he realised what had happened.

Njale's things were no longer there. Her dresses, headscarves and her white basin.

He told himself that she must have made up her mind the previous day in Mongo.

He thought of his child and he became very sad; then he saw Njale in his mind. He sat down on the edge of the bed. He saw

49

her collecting her things, putting them in the basin; Njale raving and cursing, hurrying from one end of the hut to the other, gathering her things and putting them in the basin. One after the other.

Njale, that she had left him?

No, he didn't want to believe it. To accept the fact that that was the end of their affair?

No; not with his child in her; and because he didn't want to accept the end, he found himself thinking of the beginning of their affair.

'Are you going to Mongo?' she had asked, many months ago. She was on the beach in Bwadibo and by her feet was her basin in which her things were.

'Yes,' he had replied. 'Are you going home?'

'Yes,' she said, 'I am going to your *mboka*. Will you take me?'

'Who won't take a woman like you?'

'That's it,' she said, 'Mongo, look at his face!'

'A handsome face,' he said, 'such as you will never find in the whole of Pongo.' His canoe touched the beach. 'Tell me,' he said, 'in the whole of your land, have you a young man like me?'

'Shut up,' Njale said, putting her basin in the canoe and then climbing in, 'Paddle me to Mongo if you are going to take me there,' she ordered him, her attitude mockingly haughty.

He swung the canoe away from the beach and began to paddle upstream; at first softly, and then all of a sudden he began paddling so hard that she nearly fell into the canoe.

'Who ever told you that?' she shouted at him, turning to look back.

'Sit well!' he shouted back and paddled even harder.

She had to grip both sides of the canoe with her hands to keep herself from falling either into the canoe or into the river.

'Are you mad?' she shouted, and the canoe was going almost as fast as some launches. 'Was your strength waiting for me?

Why are you going to throw me into the river?'

'I say sit well,' he said.

'A-Mongoman!'

But he wouldn't listen to her and he went on paddling very hard and the canoe was going very fast and he began to sing:

Wongele mba
Wongele mba eh
Sona muna eh.

He sang and paddled, sang and paddled, his strength and voice rejoicing and the canoe went very fast.

Then he began to slow down his paddling and she turned to face him. Sitting on one buttock she looked at him for a long time. He wasn't singing any more and he was taking his time with the paddle.

'Why are you looking at me like that?' he finally asked her.

'Don't you feel flattered that a Pongo woman as beautiful as I am is looking at your ugly face?'

'Whose face is ugly?'

'Yours,' she said. 'So you don't know how ugly you are?'

'If you say that again I'll leave you among those grasses.'

'If I say what?'

'That I, Ngos'a Mbed'a Bonam, am ugly.'

'Yes, you are ugly.'

'What?'

'I say you are ugly.'

'I'll teach you,' he said, paddling to the bushy riverbank.

'Teach me what that I haven't seen already,' she said.

The prow of the canoe bore its way through the tall grasses which grew out of the water.

He paddled forward.

'Get out of my canoe,' he snarled.

There was something hard in his voice which made her doubt

his intentions. Maybe he really meant to leave her there. A foolish Mongoman, she thought, can leave me in this jungle.

'Are you thinking of leaving me here?' she asked.

'Yes,' he said.

'Bomono will go to war against Mongo,' she said.

'Bomono?' he said, putting his paddle in the canoe.

'Yes.'

'And your husband?' he asked.

'He'll cut off your neck.'

'Now tell me the truth,' he said.

'What?'

'Are you married?'

'Why do you ask?'

He had to be careful how he went about it. What one said was very important. However, he had begun by asking her of her husband. That would be his line. He would have to pretend, just a little bit, to hear what she would say; then he would see whether or not he would have to change his tactics.

'Why I ask?' he said.

'Yes,' she said, looking him in the eyes.

'Because I have given myself a rule.'

'Which is?'

'That I'll never touch a married woman.'

'Why?'

'Because when I shall have a wife I won't want any one to touch her.'

She burst out laughing, reassured.

'You think that's how the world is?' she asked.

'Don't say that again,' he said.

'Why not?'

He didn't reply.

'But is it true that you are married?'

'Yes,' she said.

He picked up his paddle and began to paddle backwards.

'Men,' Njale laughed, sneeringly. 'You believe just anything.'

He put back the paddle in the canoe and looked at her.

'What do you say?' he asked.

'If I told you that I am not married, you'll also believe me, won't you?'

'Yes,' he said.

'All right,' she said defiantly, 'do whatever you want to do and if you don't do it, don't say it was because I am married.'

'Haven't you a husband?'

'I haven't.'

'Then let's get down.'

'To do what?'

'I say let's get down!'

'Not so loud,' she said, giving in, 'someone might be passing on the river.'

She climbed out of the canoe and stepped into the grasses, followed by him.

The sun had begun to go down and a breeze was coming from the south.

He chained the canoe to a shrub and a few paces from there he took off his loin-cloth and spread it down where the undergrowth was very sparse.

And there they knew each other intimately.

'Where is your house in Mongo?' she asked him.

He told her of his farm and she asked him if he would take her there one day.

'I don't know,' he had replied.

'You don't know.'

'Yes.'

'You think I give my body to just anybody?' she asked. 'Whether you like it or not, a-Ngoso, I'll never leave you. No matter what you do. It's the truth that I'm telling you. I'll never leave you. And take notice of the fact that I won't want you to have other women, you understand.'

He had said nothing to that and had only smiled vaguely, rather amused.

And after they had been sitting there for a long time she turned towards him and throwing her long arms about him, she asked him 'to marry' her again.

And he did.

But now where was she?

Everything she had brought with her and everything he had bought for her. She had taken all away with her.

Ngoso saw her in his imagination carrying the basin on her head through the forest which separated the farm from Bomono, her home town.

He saw the swampy stretches of jungle and dark streams.

They had once walked that road together. Today he saw her walking it alone with memories of him.

She was walking very fast, her footfalls sounding on the ground, her breasts dancing against her chest; her hips, broad as they were, swinging, the roadside undergrowth brushing against her dress as the path turned this way and then that, avoiding the huge, humped roots of great trees, thorny areas, hills and dangerous precipices. A half-dark forest reeking of the rich smell of decaying leaves and mushrooms, decaying tree-trunks and wild fruits, with the sky and the sun shut out by the branches of the tall trees.

9

'*A*-Njale!' Makole called from the beach.

Ngoso got up and went out.

Makole and his wife appeared.

'*A*-Njale,' Makole said gaily, 'haven't you heard my voice?'

Ngoso forced a smile.

'Njale,' his friend insisted, 'bring out that your ugly face.'

'But why are you standing like that?' Makole's wife asked.

Ngoso's smile broadened; but it lacked warmth.

It's not often that he looks like this, the woman told herself, he who people call 'women's Ngoso, man of joy, heady Ngoso.' No, something must be wrong.

'How?' her husband asked Ngoso when they got to the verandah.

Ngoso smiled. 'How?' he said. 'Have you arrived?'

'Yes,' the woman said, taking in her hands the basin she had been carrying on her head.

She went with it into the hut, where she put it on the table. She returned to the verandah.

'But where is Njale?' she asked.

'She's gone,' Ngoso said.

'Gone where?' Makole asked.

'She has run away to the forest.'

'No!'

'Her things are not in the house.'

'What happened?'

'I beat her.'

'Why?'

'Njale is too jealous.'

'Because of whom again was she jealous?' Makole's wife asked.

'She thinks Ewudu is my lover.'

Which Ewudu?'

'Ewud'a Pondadikalo.'

'Which Ewud'a Pondadikalo?'

'Don't you know that girl who was at Konje's place in Njopongo two years ago?'

'Ah yes,' the woman said. 'But is she a girl a man can sleep with?'

'She's now a big woman,' Makole said.

Inon looked at Ngoso. She smiled.

'So you saw her in the market?' she asked.

'No,' Ngoso said, 'in Mongo.'

'And you gave it to her?'

Ngoso laughed and went into the hut.

He returned with the calabash of palmwine. Makole sat down. Ngoso also sat down. Makole's wife remained standing.

'Bring us cups,' Ngoso said to her. 'They are on the table.'

The woman brought the cups and gave one to Ngoso and one to her husband.

'And you say you gave her her own one there,' the woman said, looking at Ngoso.

Like all women she liked that kind of talk. It was exciting because it was direct and naked.

'I didn't touch her,' Ngoso said.

'That girl is straight,' Makole said.

'Then what was she doing there?' the woman pressed on.

Ngoso filled up Makole's cup, then his. Inon didn't bring one for herself.

Makole tasted the palmwine and then drank. He drank half

the cup; then he emptied it, saying to himself that the wine was very good.

'Who asked you to be a judge?' he asked his wife as Ngoso was filling up his cup again.

'I am only asking,' she said.

'I hear that girl turned out to be very wayward,' Makole observed.

'So it looks,' Ngoso said.

'But what made Njale think that you've been there?' asked Makole's wife.

'Ewudu was in Mbongo's house while I too was there.'

'Ewudu,' Makole said, 'what a pretty girl!'

'Ngoso, pour a little for me,' the woman said.

'A little what?' Makole asked.

'Palmwine.'

'Palmwine,' her husband said, raising his cup to his mouth.

Ngoso gave his cup to Makole's wife.

'Now be careful,' Ngoso's friend said as the woman was tasting the wine. 'If my child gets drunk in your belly what will you say?'

'It won't get drunk,' she said, and drank just a little bit of the wine.

'It won't get drunk,' her husband said. 'It won't get drunk. Is that what they told you?'

He emptied his second cup.

'Take,' the woman said, holding the cup to Ngoso, her face wearing a sour look. 'It's too strong.'

'You don't know what is good,' her husband said.

'So because she quarrelled with you for having been in Mbongo's place with Ewudu that was why you beat her?'

'That wasn't why I beat her.'

'Why then did you beat her?'

'Who!' said Makole, 'looks like he asked her for something

57

and she refused. But if you knew you had beaten her why did you say we should come?'

'Yes,' his wife asked Ngoso, 'why did you call us when you knew full well that you had annoyed her?'

'He wanted us to come and see how more beautiful her face had become after the beating. You, daylight! You have the whole night and still . . . Once a woman is pregnant, you can't add another child on the first one, *a*-daylight, if it's another child you are already looking for.'

'*A, a*-Makole,' Ngoso said.

Husband and wife exchanged indulgent glances and Ngoso frowned at the thought that Njale had gone away.

They ate the food Inon had brought.

That night, as Ngoso lay alone in his bed, unable to go to sleep, he thought it would be wrong for him to rush to Bomono. Njale might think he had come to beg her. That was something a man should never do, beg a woman. If there were men who did it, he Ngos'a Mbed'a Bonam wasn't one of them.

One week after Njale's departure the sun was again so bright and its heat so intense that it was clear that was going to be the last really sunny day of the year.

And so it turned out to be; for, in the afternoon, a shadow suddenly fell over the forest and the river and the winds were reluctant and rather chilly.

Mountains of clouds rose in the north where the Mungo River has its source, and towards the evening the sky rumbled in the north, announcing the first floods of the year, the sound of water as those northern thunderstorms were called here in the south.

Ngoso thought of the sweet potatoes his lover Ndongo had planted. She had come from Bojongo during the planting season and it had been impossible for her to get on with Njale. The two women even fought; and immediately after the planting was over Ndongo had to return to Bojongo.

Her farm, like the sweet potato farms of most women, was in Ngole. Njale too had planted sweet potatoes; but because she didn't get on with other women she had planted her potatoes on Ngoso's farm, just outside his hut, and had harvested them some five days before the day he beat her. It was as if even then she had known she would be leaving him. It had been a poor harvest.

As soon as they had heard the sound of water women and their children hurried to Ngole. Flood water spoilt potatoes; so they had to be harvested before the river rose to the level of the potato fields.

The harvesting was hectic. There was a lot of canoe-movement on the river as the potatoes were being transported from Ngole to the other bank and from there to the village. Women and their children worked late and by the time night fell many plots were still unharvested. And Ngoso worried about Ndongo's farm.

By the following morning the river had changed its colour. The water had become slightly chalky and very cold. And like the previous day, many canoes were on the river because of the harvest.

Ngoso talked to Muyao about Ndongo's farm. The young woman got three girls, and Mbedi paddled them to Ngole where they harvested Ndongo's potatoes and transported them to Ngoso's hut.

But the river didn't after all rise as high as they had feared. In fact it didn't rise to what could be called the first flood. Maybe the rain had been very slight in the north, some people thought.

Makole's sister-in-law, Longe, had come from Mongo to help Inon with the harvest.

'Ewudu is a very bad girl,' she said one evening when Ngoso went to their place. 'They say she fought with her sister just because she said she shouldn't be friends with a Bamoun woman who sells her body for money. They say before coming to Mongo she wasn't staying with her any more.'

'How is the world like that?' Makole's wife wondered. 'That girl used to be so quiet. I remember when she was in Njopongo —'

'Ewudu is another thing now,' her sister said.

'I met her on the beach two days ago,' Makole said, 'you should have heard the smart talk which was coming out of that girl's mouth. "*Uweh, a*-Makole!" she said as if we were of the same age group. "How is Inon? They say she is pregnant. *Aye!* All people are having children with the exception of myself." I looked at the mouth which was saying all that and told myself that if only one would slap it!'

'She's real fire, that girl,' his sister-in-law said.

'When she asked me how Ngoso was and I told her that because of her Njale had run away to the forest,' Makole went on, 'she simply made faces —'

'*E-e!*'

'And asked: "Which Njale?" I told her she was Ngoso's woman. "But is that any load?" she asked.'

'Listen to that!' Makole's wife said. 'But what brings about such things?'

'In Mongo they are already calling her the disrupter of marriages.'

'*Na!*' Makole's wife said. 'Mongo that isn't lacking in epithets.'

'But Ngoso is sitting as if all this talk doesn't concern him,' Makole's sister-in-law said.

'What do you want me to say?'

'But after all things have been said,' Makole said, 'one must confess that that girl is straight.'

'Yes,' Inon's sister admitted. 'Ewudu is pretty. Who knows whether it is her beauty which has made her so drunk.'

'About that one,' Ngoso said, 'let Njale do whatever she likes, I Ngoso will know what is there.'

10

'*E-e*,' Ebanda said as Ngoso was paddling into the beach in Mongo.

He was on his way to Mudeka Market with a canoe-load of plantains.

'Look at his face,' Ebanda added.

Ngoso didn't say anything.

'*A*-Ngoso,' Jongo said. He was on the beach with Esobe, Ebanda, Mulobe, Eyabe and Dibobe la Kombo. They were sitting on the backs of over-turned canoes under the huge mango tree. Eyabe was making a throw-net. 'Hasn't the woman left you?' Jongo added.

'*A*-Ngoso,' Dibobe said.

'Njale said easy,' Jongo pursued, 'but you wouldn't listen. Give me some rest. But where? You. Hasn't she gone away at last?'

Ngoso smiled, paddling calmly and thinking of Ewudu.

'He laughs,' Dibobe said.

'Njale said easy,' Jongo la Bopula resumed, 'but where?'

'Because Ngos'a Mbedi has decided not to fight any more,' Ngoso said, putting his paddle in the canoe, 'is that why you all are so drunk?'

'Alight!' Jongo challenged him more in jest than in earnest

even though Jongo was just as heady as Ngoso. 'I'll make you eat mud.'

'Whose Ngoso?' Ngoso asked.

'Ngos'a Mbedi.'

'Not a single day.'

'I say alight!'

Ngoso alighted and in mock fury walked up to Jongo. But Dibobe quickly interposed himself between them.

'Who ever told you that?' he asked Ngoso. 'Did they say it was Jongo who asked Njale to run away to the forest?'

And they laughed exuberantly and cracked more jokes; then Eyabe asked if Makole wasn't going to come down.

'Tomorrow,' Ngoso said. 'Do you know if Mbongo is at home?'

'Your brother has gone to Kongwe,' Esobe said.

'I'm coming,' Ngoso said. 'I'll stretch my feet to the town.' He met Njale's friend Etaka on her verandah, tying *miondo*.

'Now is it right, what you did?' she asked when she saw him.

'What isn't right?'

'What you did to Njale.'

'Where is your husband?'

'He's in Kongwe. He went with Mbongo. How is Longe?'

'She's well.'

'Inon?'

'She's well.'

'Makole?'

'He's well.'

'But won't you sit down?'

'Why not?'

'Haven't you heard from Njale?' she asked after Ngoso had sat down.

'No,' he said. 'Say, Etaka, do you know if Ewudu is still there?'

'She's gone.'

'Where?'

'Where? Didn't they tell you she had a man?'

'That talk is not for me,' he said.

'Why?' she asked. 'Because it's she that you now want?'

'I didn't say so.'

'Go and persuade Njale to return. Don't throw away our child.'

'Etaka, never. Throw my child away? Not a single day. Ours is ours.'

'So go and bring her back.'

'You really mean Ewudu is gone?'

'It's the truth I'm telling you. Go and ask.'

'Ugh.'

'What's the matter?'

'I wanted to see her.'

'You too want her?'

'Why?'

'No,' the woman said. 'I only asked.'

'That Ewudu because of whom Njale nearly killed herself.'

'And because of whom you are killing yourself.'

'*A*,' he said. 'Who told you that?'

'No one,' Etaka said. 'I too just said it. She's on the way. It's this very afternoon that they left.'

'They?'

'Yes. With your lover Jengu.'

'That talk is no longer straight.'

'Why?'

'Do you know whether she'll go straight to that her man or whether she'll be in the market tomorrow?'

'From what I heard them saying it looks as though she'll sleep in Mudeka tonight.'

'Good.'

'Good? I say is it her you now want?'

'I love her very much.'

'Don't say that again,' Etaka said. 'Marry Njale. We love her in spite of her ugly face. Leave Ewudu alone. She's war itself.'

'How?'

'The things that girl did here! I'm telling you that she shook Mongo *ná puku puku*.'

'And I want to shake her.'

'She's in Mudeka.'

I I

He got to Mudeka very late in the evening.

He put his paddle in the canoe, sat back and relaxed.

The market was on the hillside overlooking the waterfront. Fishermen were in their canoes as well as farmers like Ngoso. And the waterfront was a bit noisy and there were lanterns.

He got up, took his paddle and travelling bag and raising his loin-cloth, stepped into the water and waded to the shore where, putting down the paddle and bag, he chained the canoe, then he took the paddle and the bag and turned towards the market and walked through it to the town.

He knocked on Esadi's door with the knuckles of his right hand. There was silence. He knocked again, a little harder.

'Who is that?' Jengu's voice asked.

'Ngoso.'

He heard her footsteps hurrying to the door where she began to struggle with the bolt.

'But the useless door won't open,' Jengu cried. '*A*-Ngoso, you thought of us at last because Njale has gone away, isn't it?'

'Open the door,' he said roughly.

'But what is wrong with this useless door?'

'That's no reason why you should shout,' Ngoso heard Ewudu's voice. 'Ngoso, Ngoso,' she said, clearly drawing attention to herself, 'so people won't hear again.'

'Oh this door,' Jengu said.

'Lift it a bit,' her sister said. 'You have even forgotten that one must lift it in order to open it. *Aye!*'

'Since she has heard her man's voice,' Ewudu said.

'Don't provoke me,' Jengu said. She sounded very excited. 'This door!'

'If you are trembling like that,' Ewudu said, 'how do you think your hands will ever be firm on the bolt?'

'It's my man who is outside,' Jengu said, smiling at her sister and Ewudu. Then she went on struggling with the door.

'I say lift it!'

'But I am lifting it,' Jengu said helplessly. 'Isn't it the door that I am lifting like this?'

Then all of a sudden the bolt fell back and Jengu held the door open.

A lantern was in the centre of the room.

Ngoso greeted them. The three women replied. He shook Jengu's hand and then she turned and pushed the door shut.

'Give me the bag,' she said.

He leaned his paddle against the wall. Jengu took the bag to her room.

Esadi's legs were stretched out in front of her. Ewudu's were bent double, her thighs against her chest. Her small face looked even prettier tonight. He shook her hand, then Esadi's.

'How are you?' he asked Jengu's sister.

'We are well,' the woman replied with her usual air of indifference.

She was like that until she lost her temper. Then she shouted all over the place.

Her sister Jengu was very nice. She now came out of the room, a lamp in her hand. She noticed Ngoso was preoccupied. Something was on his mind. Maybe he was thinking of that Pongo woman. Yes, especially as she's pregnant. A little envy touched her heart. But it passed. I'll talk to him about her later, she told herself, when the two of us will be in the room.

'*Na!*' Esadi said. 'We are very rich — two lamps in the same room. Your man has brought us a whole tin of kerosene.'

'Haven't I just lit it?' her sister said, frowning.

'But what difference does that make?' Esadi asked. 'Was it water you put in it or kerosene?'

Jengu's countenance darkened. 'As if it's because of those few drops of kerosene that we shall no longer be rich.'

'All right,' her sister said. 'I said your man has brought us a whole tin of kerosene.'

'Ngoso,' Jengu said, 'are you hungry?'

'What have you in the house?'

'There is some sauce,' she said, 'and *miondo*. But I don't like those *miondo*. I'd rather cook a little pepper soup for you.'

'Quick.'

Jengu unbolted the back door and went out.

The lamp she had with her consisted of a bottle which had once contained vaseline. A little kerosene was now in it. A hole had been struck through the lid and through this the end of a cloth wick had been stuck. The rest of the wick was soaked in the kerosene. A swaying, soot-coated flame danced on the lid and

66

as soon as she had opened the door she cupped her right hand about the lid to shelter the flame against the wind.

'Ugh!' they heard her cry.

'Has the wind put out the light?' Ewudu asked.

'Yes,' Jengu moaned. But she didn't return to relight the lamp. After a while they heard her splitting firewood.

'With that darkness,' her sister said.

'With that darkness,' Ewudu repeated after her, looking up at Ngoso without taking off her chin from her knees on which it was resting. She was sitting on a low stool.

'Now that she has seen her man her whole thing is erect, trembling.'

'Since we all are now grown up,' Ngoso said, 'that's the way to talk.'

Ewudu looked at him as if she found him simply amusing.

He felt he couldn't return alone to his farm and he imagined himself returning with Ewudu. The creeks immediately after Mudeka; the mudskippers swimming in and out of the salt water.

The sea. The wind. The waves and the mangrove trees. The birds of the horizon and the sea bird flying just over the dancing waves. And he and Ewudu conversing. And in the distance baobabs.

After the sea more creeks, and then the Mungo River lined with raffia palm trees; more mangrove trees with their long, over-hanging roots.

He longed to have Ewudu as his wife. He loved her. Their eyes met over the lantern.

'I am seeing,' Jengu's sister said.

'What are you seeing?' Ngoso asked her.

'Nothing,' the woman said, 'since I haven't eyes.'

Ewudu yawned.

Jengu came in. She went into the room. And presently they heard her hit her leg against an iron pot.

67

'*Ate!*' she cried.

'Have you wounded yourself?' Ngoso asked.

'No,' she said even though she couldn't be sure just then for the room was dark.

'But why don't you come and take the lamp?' Ewudu asked, her eyes looking sleepy. She sat up.

'Ewudu, no,' her friend Jengu said.

She came out of the room, an iron pot in her hands. She went with it to the kitchen in the backyard where she had made a fire.

'Ewudu,' Ngoso said. 'I brought a bunch of plantains for Jengu. Take a tray."

She frowned and was going to protest when their eyes met again, very discreetly and she understood. But she was worried about Jengu's sister. Wouldn't she suspect? Already she had said she was seeing. But what can that do, she thought, rising.

Ngoso got up and went out.

She took a tray and joined him outside.

I 2

'Ewudu,' he said as they were walking towards the waterfront. 'It won't be right that you'll grow old without my having known you.'

'But whose fault would it be?'

He put his arm round her. 'This your small waist,' he said. She looked back. 'She's cooking,' he said, 'if it's Jengu you are looking for.'

They both laughed.

He took off his arm from her waist.

Men in swishing loin-cloths walked past, some going to, others returning from, the waterfront. Women conversed gaily with the men. It was a great night, the eve of market day.

'Where are we going?' she asked.

'As if you don't know,' he said.

They got to the market, turned left and walked down an alley lined with shanty stalls. Here and there a lantern shone, dimly. Here and there a trader dozed against the bales of cloth he would be selling the following morning, or against a huge crate containing his wares.

Down the alley, on Ngoso's right, people were gathered around a woman who sold fried ripe plantains with fried fish. The smell of the plantains and the fish in the sizzling oil was mixed with the slimy smell of salt water creeks with their fish and mud-skippers and the breath of the sea.

The customers sounded gay about the woman and she shouted and laughed, joking with them, and they laughed and shouted. They will be there, all night, eating ripe plantains with fried fish and talking in a carefree manner until the morning when the market will open.

As Ngoso and Ewudu walked down the alley they saw some people get up and walk out of the woman's stall and others going into it. Some of them sat down. Others remained standing.

Ngoso turned left and Ewudu followed him. They walked up a slope, bent their heads and went into a stall, walked through it and then through several others.

'But is it here that your own waterfront is?' she asked, pretending she didn't know where he was taking her.

'Yes,' he said.

'Then where is your canoe, *a*-Ngoso of lies?'

They got to a rather dark stall. The light from the nearest lantern couldn't reach them and no one was in any of the adjoining stalls.

Here he took off his loin-cloth and folding it double, he spread it on the ground. Then he took off the pair of shorts he always wore under his loin-cloth whenever he was leaving his house.

'Ngoso, why do you want me?' Ewudu asked him.

He could barely see her face.

'I don't know,' he said, his thing full and pointing at her.

'Then leave me,' she said.

'No, I won't.'

'Let's go to the waterfront.'

'After.'

'Ngoso, no. Don't you know I have a man?'

'He's not your husband.'

'But he's going to be.'

'At the moment he isn't.'

'Ngoso.'

'What?' he said, putting his hands on her shoulders, and pressing her down, gently.

'Ngoso,' she said.

'What?'

'Let's go to the waterfront. You said I should come and carry plantains.'

'Yes,' he agreed.

'So let's go to your canoe. Look at the tray I brought with me. I came out because I thought you really wanted me to come and carry plantains.'

'First carry me,' he said, squeezing her shoulders tenderly.

'No, Ngoso, please.'

'Ewudu!'

'Yes?'

'Are you playing with me?'

'No.'

'Then lie down at once.'

She hesitated, looking up at him; then she dropped her look, putting down the tray.

'Jengu will know,' she said, taking off her underwear and sitting on the loin-cloth, having raised her dress. 'Eh, Ngoso, she'll know.'

'I know,' he said, raising her dress higher and lowering himself on her. 'So what do you want me to do?'

'Leave me,' she said, parting her thighs.

'I have heard.'

'Ngoso.'

'What?'

'I say leave me,' she said, parting her thighs a little more. 'I can't do this to Jengu. Ngoso, truly, leave me, please.'

Her voice was warm and intimate and it was inviting him.

He pushed her gently to make her lie on her back; but she wouldn't, pretending, still resisting feebly, beautifully because actually she wasn't resisting.

'Lie down,' he whispered urgently. 'Ewudu, quick.'

'Ngoso, leave me,' she gasped, leaning back and opening herself.

'Yes,' he found himself saying, all his body taut with desire. 'Then?'

'Put,' he said, all his life now wanting to feel her wet warmth, the depth of her womanhood. 'Ewudu, *wele*, put. Ewudu — '

'Ngoso,' she gasped, hesitating, excited, thrilled.

'Quick!' He couldn't wait any longer. 'Ewudu!'

And as if reluctantly, she put her left hand between them.

'Ngoso, please leave me,' she begged, her hand closing on his thing. It was warm and she liked the feel of it in the palm of her hand.

71

'Ewudu,' he said with love.

'Ngoso,' she replied, introducing him into the lustfulness of her life. And then she wrapped her arms around him.

He sank with an effort, pushing forward, upwards.

'Ewudu,' he whispered, withdrawing and then pushing in again. 'Ewudu — '

'Ngoso leave me,' she groaned. 'Ngoso ... Ngoso ... Ngoso ... Ngoso. Eh? Ngoso, eh?' And she was spinning and spinning her waist. 'Ngoso, I say leave me, 'she went on telling him. 'I say leave me, Ngoso.' And she was shaking her waist, spinning it, withdrawing and then bearing herself towards him again ....

She held him very tight, taking and taking him and giving him access to the very profound end of her womanhood; and then his thing struck the entrance to her womb.

That caused her so much unbearable pleasure and pain that the perplexing process of satisfaction immediately took control of her.

She clawed him. Ungripped him, then clawed him again, tightened her hold about him and then she was clawing him again and she was groaning and grunting and swallowing, clawing his back and sides, crying, and he was at her, furiously loading her with pleasure and joy.

He held her tight, her movement under him becoming a series of rapid upward and downward jerks and she felt as if he was a storm. The more she moved, the deeper she took him and the more she enjoyed it.

'Ngoso, Ngoso,' she cried. 'Ngoso, *na ki kwa*; I am falling.'

And she tightened her embrace about him even more violently and then her voice changed, becoming tiny and funny and laboured, very deep in her as she became exhausted, her embrace relaxing. 'I have fallen,' she moaned feebly, sighing and her arms slumped on the loin-cloth.

But although he had made her secret ecstasy he still hadn't poured the drops of his own pleasure into her. He was still strong and he turned over so that they lay side by side while he waited for her to rest.

She was peaceful, lying there with him, on the loin-cloth, while in the distance the town talked and laughed, drinking, boasting, gossiping, despairing and hoping.

But the market seemed really peaceful, anticipating the following day and its buying and selling.

The crowd of customers who were gathered around the woman who sold fried ripe plantains laughed from time to time and some of them swore.

Njale's bold face loomed in his mind. But he brushed aside the thought.

Then he began to touch Ewudu's breasts in order to excite her again and it was easy because he was still in her, strong and straight and presently he was on her again and he was saying to himself that it was because, yes, because, because of women that life was really good, yes, really good.

'Yes!' he said aloud and then he could think no more.

A long time of uninterrupted rhythmic action passed, the clapping of waist against waist and Ewudu began to feel once more as if she had been pushed and pushed and pushed to the sky of all intimate dreams from which she was now falling through clouds and thunderstorms, such an intense sensation, such incredible pleasure.

And he moaned with her and she felt as if she was falling eternally and she wept, her face wet with tears and he pressed himself to her as if he wanted to enter and live in her. And she moaned and moaned, calling his name until she could no longer articulate words and was only breathing dreamily through her mouth which she had left open.

And then she felt she was on the earth again under him and

73

it occured to her that in spite of all the pain which had preceded the pleasure he hadn't hurt her; only that tiredness, that fine exhaustion, the feeling of having been battered and crushed by storms and then she realised that although he was still on her he too had fallen; he had fallen into her pleasure.

'*O ma kwa?*' she asked him, caressing his back and sides. 'Have you fallen?'

'*E,*' he said, satisfied.

I 3

'If you knew what I am thinking,' she said as they were going to his canoe.

'What are you thinking?'

'If my man should hear about it,' she said, 'he'll beat me to death.'

Ekema was like that. He beat her the day following the afternoon they met. That was because he had seen her talking to a man. That was outside Esadi's house. As soon as the man had strolled away, Ekema called Ewudu and asked her what she had been discussing with him.

'Nothing,' she had replied and before she could say another word his palm had hit her mouth.

The following market day he beat her again in Esadi's house; so that when Ewudu told Jengu that she was going to live with

Ekema in the plantation camp, Ngoso's lover had found it difficult to understand why Ewudu was going to do that. Later, however, she thought that maybe Ekema was like Ngoso in intimacy.

'Truly?' Ngoso asked.

'Truly,' Ewudu said. 'If Ekema hears what you have done —'

He laughed. 'Say what *we* have done,' he said.

'*Na*!' she said. 'What *we* have done — as if I wanted it. I only did it because you wanted it.'

'What a woman!'

'Sincerely.'

The persistent noise of the people who were waiting for the morning on the waterfront contained some laughter and quite a bit of swearing. And the freshness of the sea breeze felt good on the face and arms, especially after one had just been sweating.

Tomorrow there will be a large crowd in the market and on the waterfront many canoes. People will come from the north. And from Mongo, in canoes. Some will come overland from Missaka through Muquo and Mwanda. Others will come in canoes.

Even from Mongo some people will come overland through Kongwe. And men and women will come from many other villages.

Workers will come from the plantation camps. Traders from Missellele; others as far as from Tiko.

Fishermen from the fishing ports.

There will be many canoes on the waterfront. Many were already there for some canoemen, like Ngoso, when he wasn't accompanied by a woman, preferred to arrive on the eve of market day.

'You think I still have the strength to carry any load on this my head?' Ewudu asked, when they got to his canoe.

He didn't reply as he bent forward, removed a plantain leaf and then lifted a large bunch of plantains which he put on the shore; then he lifted another one and put it down besides the first one; and after replacing the leaf he turned towards her.

'Ngoso,' she began, hanging her head. 'I cant't. . . . '

'Carry it if you are going to carry it,' he said coarsely.

He put the smaller of the two bunches in the tray and taking it in both hands he put it on her head; then, taking the other bunch with one hand, they started up the hill.

'Why don't you come and rest on the farm for a few days?' he suggested.

'What will Jengu say?'

'Jengu is not my wife.'

When they got to the house and he knocked on the door they got no reply. He knocked again. Still no one answered. He lost his temper and banged his fist on the door so hard that the whole house shook.

'What's the matter?' Esadi's indignant voice rang out. 'I say what is the matter? What have I done that my house is being knocked down?'

They heard her open the door of her room and then she was opening the front door. She struggled with the bolt briefly and then she opened the door and walked back to her room the door of which she shut and bolted as soon as she had entered.

Ngoso and Ewudu went in. The bottle lamp Jengu had lit was on the floor, shining dimly.

Ewudu put down the tray and massaged her neck, stretching it because the bunch of plantains was heavy.

Ngoso crossed over to the door of Jengu's room. He put down his bunch of plantains and then, boum, boum, boum, he knocked on the door.

'Jengu,' he called, 'Jengu.'

Boum, boum, boum, he knocked.

'Jengu!' he thundered. 'Jengu, open the door.'

'But what's the matter?' Ewudu asked, highly embarrassed.

'Jengu, we only went to the waterfront to carry plantains,' she added.

'Shut up,' her friend cried her down from the other side of the door. 'Who asked you to explain to me where you went? You brought your waywardness right here. You aren't even ashamed with your useless *mbamba*.'

'But what have I done?' Ewudu asked, trembling for Jengu was her best friend. I told Ngoso, she thought, but he wouldn't listen. 'Jengu,' she said, 'now why are you angry?'

'Shut up!' Jengu said heatedly. 'Your bag is there.' That was when Ewudu and Ngoso noticed that a packed travelling bag was leaning against the wall near the front door. 'Take it and go to wherever you like. What have I done, what have I done; because you left children here you can fool.'

'Jengu,' Ngoso said menacingly, 'are you opening the door or not?'

'I won't open it until that thing goes away,' she said, yielding to the power his manliness excercised over her. 'Her bag is there. All her things are in it.'

'All right,' Ewudu said, 'since it has come to that, I have gone.'

'Yes go,' Jengu said.

'You are wasting your time,' Ewudu said sneeringly. She thought of Epossi whose house was the only other place she could sleep in Mudeka. 'You think if I want to have something to do with Ngoso it is what you are saying there that will stop me? You make me laugh.'

She went and picked up her bag.

'Have you a place to sleep?' Ngoso asked her.

'What about all the men she has in Mudeka?' Jengu said maliciously.

'I'll go and see if Epossi will let me in,' Ewudu said. 'To-morrow.'

He followed her with his look as she was going out.

Jengu opened the door, came out into the parlour and went and bolted the front door.

'You are laughing,' she said when she turned to face him.

'What came into your head?' he said. 'What do you think I did with Ewudu?'

'Nothing,' Jengu's elder sister Esadi answered from the other room. 'What does she think you did with Ewudu since I hadn't eyes to see the eyes you were making at each other.'

'Ngoso,' Jengu said. 'Why did you do that?'

He shrugged his shoulders and went into the room and sat on the bed.

'Where is the food you prepared?' he asked when Jengu came in with the lamp.

'First answer me,' she said, putting the lamp down. 'Why did you do that?'

'Do what?'

'What you know you did.'

'Did you say you didn't finally cook anything?'

'I asked you a question.'

But he only smiled in a way that made her feel that he was slighting her. This was too much for her. He was laughing at her, she thought, because of that useless Ewudu!

She swung round in a fit of hysteria and collapsed against the wall on her right and sobbed into the thatches.

'Please don't knock down my house,' her sister croaked.

Jengu sobbed, the whole of her back shaking until Ngoso got up and, putting his arms around her, pulled her to the bed.

He made her sit on the edge of the bed and she found his arms about her very comforting, very reassuring. She took his hold about her as a sign that he still cared for her.

When she calmed down, she got up, her shoulders sagging, and crossed over to a corner of the room where her pots were. She felt the lid of one of them with the back of her hand.

'Is it cold?' he asked.

She nodded. 'I'll warm it,' she mumbled.

'*A*,' he said. 'Give it to me like that.'

'I say it is cold,' she said and went out with the pot.

Ngoso stretched himself across the bed and closing his eyes he thought of tomorrow and the days after tomorrow. And that meant thinking of Ewudu.

He recalled all the bad things he had heard said about her. Disrupter of marriages. There was some truth in that, for he realized Njale just didn't matter any more to him. Of course she wasn't his wife; but she was going to become his wife for he had been thinking seriously of marrying her.

But now he wasn't sure any more. He wanted to marry Ewudu. Then he thought of what Njale's friend in Mongo had said about Ewudu only that afternoon. And he had said he wanted to shake her; but there he was, shaken by her charm. No matter what happened, he decided, he would take her from her man.

A few moments later he heard Jengu enter.

'There's water for you in the bathroom,' she said.

He understood why she had done that. He wished, without meaning it, she could also arrange for Ewudu to be washed away from his thoughts. Then he suddenly found it disturbing that he was thinking of marrying her.

He went to the backyard where the bathroom was and had his bath after which he returned to the room and sitting on the edge of the bed, oiled himself with *mananga*.

Then she set an old crate before him. She served him his meal, a dish of cocoyams and hot pepper soup cooked with dried fish. She put the dishes on the empty crate.

When he finished oiling his arms, legs and thighs, and rubbing his hands on his face and combing his bushy hair, he ate.

After the meal he flushed his mouth, spat the water in a corner of the room and went out to breathe the night air.

When he returned to the room he couldn't resist her from the way she was looking at him. And because his desire was generous he was soon on her, pacifying her noisily with the weight of his manhood, the wooden bed creaking, and she forgot everything about Ewudu. It was as if she had never known her; as if Ngoso hadn't wronged her that very evening.

'*Bo!a*-Jengu!' she thought she heard her sister rebuke her from the adjoining room. 'After what he has just done! *Bo*, you are an animal. *Aye*!'

The night was slightly windy as he turned round outside their house and wished her goodnight, saying she should sleep well. She wished him the same, still wet from his love.

'Now,' she added, 'don't go to Epossi's house.'

'Tomorrow,' he said evasively.

'Do you hear?' she said.

'Yes. Come to the waterfront in the morning.'

'*O*,' she said. 'Tomorrow.'

As he started off he heard her locking the door.

The night had grown less noisy for it was getting late and few people were still outside.

He walked very fast. He went to Epossi's house and knocked on the door.

'Enter,' Ewudu said when she opened the door.

He went in and put his travelling bag down. He leaned his paddle against the wall and then sat down at a table on which a lamp stood.

'I thought you'd sleep there,' she said.

'No,' he said. 'I can't leave that canoe like that.'

'I told you they'd know,' she said.

'But what can that do?' he said. 'Where is Epossi?'

'She's gone out.'

'Will she sleep out?'

'No. She'll be back,' Ewudu said and then sitting opposite him and spreading her arms on the table, she sighed and began to think of her life.

'Ngoso,' she said, looking up.

'Yes?'

'I can't return to Ekema. If he knows what I have done, I don't know what he will do.'

'Now you don't know,' he said. 'I thought you said he will kill you?'

'Don't think I am joking.'

'No, you are not.'

'Yes,' she said. 'I can't return to his place.'

'I told you you could come to the farm.'

'I can't return to Ekema,' she repeated, looking at her hands which were clasped together on the table.

'Is that any load? Tomorrow we are gone.'

'But I can't leave my things in his place.'

'We shall go and take them tomorrow after the market.'

She looked at him. 'If he sees you?' she asked.

'I am not afraid of him,' he said.

'If you knew Ekema you wouldn't be saying that.'

'Shut up,' he said, getting up.

'Sit down,' she said.

'No,' he said, 'I am going.'

'You are going?'

'Yes,' he said. 'I told you I have to get back to the canoe.'

'So what have we decided?'

'We are going up tomorrow,' he said, sitting down.

'I know. But. . . .'

'But what? Don't you want to go up with me?'

'I didn't say that.'

'Then?'

'But his mother.'

'Whose mother?'

'Ekema's,' she said. 'He took me to her last month. Ngoso, you should have seen that woman. When we were about to leave she took him to a corner and they talked. I don't know what she said to him; but when they came in to join me, she held his hand and mine together and asked Ekema not to treat me lightly; she even asked him to marry me, saying she thought I was the right woman for him; and when she asked me if I would marry her son I said yes. Ngoso, believe me that at the time I didn't think I should ever want to leave him. But now. . . .'

He thought he heard footsteps on the verandah and when they weren't followed by a knock on the door he got up and went and opened the window. He looked out. He saw no one.

'I heard as if there was someone outside,' he said, shutting the window.

He returned to his chair.

'I don't know what I am going to do.'

'Don't worry yourself,' he said, 'you'll come with me to-morrow!'

'But my things?'

'We shall go and take them. Haven't you a friend at the camp? Which camp in fact?'

She told him the name of the camp.

'A friend?' she said.

'Yes.'

'There's a Bakweri woman.'

'What is the number of her room?'

She told him. 'Why?'

'We shall go together and I'll wait for you at her place while you make preparations. You may even find a girl who will carry your things if Ekema is not at home. She will go ahead and you'll meet her on the way and I will come after. Is your friend married?'

'Yes,' Ewudu said. 'But her husband and Ekema aren't on good terms. They don't speak to each other.'

'So you see,' he said, rising. 'Everything is all right. Tomorrow meet me at the blacksmith's place at the end of the town. Around two o'clock.'

'But won't I see you before that time?'

'If you wish,' he said. 'Come to the waterfront.'

He took his bag and then his paddle.

'Tomorrow,' he said.

But as he was stepping outside he saw Jengu walking away, her hands behind her clasped over her buttocks; head down.

He didn't call her. He didn't even feel angry because she had been eavesdropping on their conversation for he recognised the fact that once more he had betrayed her devotion to him. But he couldn't help it. He had left his heart between Ewudu's thighs. He saw himself going to the plantation camp with her the following afternoon. He saw himself beating up her man and all the workers shouting as if it was a wrestling match. Then he and Ewudu were leaving the camp and the workers were calling him names. Some were calling him, 'foolish man who steals away other people's women,' and he imagined them abusing Ewudu, some calling her a prostitute just as Njale had done.

He walked faster.

That night it drizzled towards dawn.

14

In the morning the buying and selling began. The thatched stalls of the market were like giant mushrooms growing on a hill that leaned against the horizon.

The market was crowded. It was noisy. Boisterous haggling.

Ngoso sold his plantains and the sun rose.

Colourful dresses. Men and women. Noise and shouting and laughter. Noisy haggling and the sun rose higher and higher, heightening the gaiety and the colours of the market, assuring the first build-up of the day's heat.

Some of the men were dressed in shirts and trousers; some even in jackets, and many wore felt hats. But most of the men from the coast wore loin-cloths, like Ngoso, and shirts, and some wore felt hats too.

Many people from the northern grasslands wore their fine home-made loosely-fitting shirts which were richly embroidered. Some wore them over loin-cloths which weren't as large as those, the *sanja*, worn by southerners. Others wore the embroidered shirts over pairs of shorts; and others still over trousers.

Heating up the waterfront, the sun intensified the odours of the market. The smell of fish, dried and fresh fish, invaded the air.

Ngoso sold his plantains and searched for Ewudu with his eyes, glancing at the milling crowds, wondering why she still hadn't come.

Once more he had the impression that something terrible was going to happen to him. He hated to imagine the day he and Ewudu would part company, when the joy and the intimate contact of their bodies last night would have no other significance but that of an adventure towards the permanence of happiness. A frustrated dream.

He hoped he wouldn't have to regret having met her. He was anxious. It wasn't often that he was anxious. And still he knew she loved him.

It was a great market day. Pepper and other spices and various foodstuffs, cooked and raw. Meat and dried game meat.

The scent of patent medicines and of camphor. The smell of bales of cloth.

Alligator pepper and many other medicinal spices.

Palm oil and other oils.

The sky clouded. People raised their eyes to the heavens, fearing it was going to rain.

It didn't, for a wind rose from the sea behind the mangrove trees and cleared the sky of its rainclouds and the sun appeared again. But it wasn't as bright as it had been earlier on.

Muslims sitting cross-legged on floor mats sold paltry wares among which were fishing hooks, twine and other sizes of fishing line as well as rings, cheap watches, ear-rings, leather sandals, slippers and perfume; and they sold and chewed cola-nuts. They always had cola-nuts in their mouths. It reddened their lips and they chewed and chewed, almost imperceptibly and they looked very solemn about it.

And then Ngoso heard that Njale had died! It was a woman who brought the news from Bomono.

'A-Ngoso,' she said when she emerged from the crowd. She looked very sad, very miserable. She was the youngest of Njale's many aunts. 'Are you in this market?'

'Yes,' he replied.

'So you didn't hear that your wife died?'

'My wife?'

'Njale.'

'You are joking,' he said, smiling.

She looked at him and the sadness in her eyes was profound; it was tinged with anger which she was trying to control. Ngoso had always known that she liked him.

The smile left his face because of what he saw in the woman's eyes.

She was the only one in their family who wanted Njale to marry him. The others preferred a rich trader in Penja who was madly in love with Njale.

'She died two days ago,' the woman said. 'We buried her yesterday.'

'And you didn't send anyone to come and tell me?'

'And we didn't send anyone to come and tell you,' she repeated after him contemptuously. 'Who killed her?'

'I must go to Bomono,' he said gravely.

The woman looked at him in silence for a long time; then she sighed and shook her head sadly and went back into the market.

Soon afterwards Ewudu appeared.

'What happened?' she asked, looking into his anguished face.

Without looking at her he told her what the woman had just told him.

'Uweh!' she cried, clapping her hands, sincerely shaken even though she had never met Njale personally. But with Etaka and Jengu and Mwato they had discussed her in Mongo only yesterday. 'Uweh!' she said, still clapping her hands. 'We called her name in Mongo yesterday not knowing that she was already dead.'

'Go and bring Epossi,' he said, fed up with the world. 'I'll put aside two bunches of plantains for her.'

Just then the woman who had brought the news came towards them.

'Don't go to Bomono,' she said to Ngoso. 'They'll kill you.'

'I'll go.'

'Ngoso, take my advice. You don't know how they feel about

86

you. Everybody thinks it's the beating you gave her that killed her. She miscarried just after she arrived. She suffered a lot.'

'I'll go to Bomono,' he said. 'Why won't I go?'

She sighed and shook her head.

'Maybe I shouldn't have warned you,' she said gloomily. 'I ought to have known that with your headstrongness fear of death won't stop you from going. But if you still love your life, take my advice. Don't go. It's not your going that will resurrect her.'

She left them.

'Go and bring Epossi,' Ngoso said.

Ewudu sighed and left and Ngoso sold a few more bunches of plantains.

Then the two women returned. Epossi was tall and slim with a long neck and a bulky, undulating bosom. She hadn't any children even though the whole of her bosom seemed to be full of nothing else but milk.

'*Uweh!*' she too exclaimed, clapping her hands as Ewudu had been doing only a while ago. "What sadness!'

'Epossi leave me,' Ngoso said. 'It's nothing to talk about.'

'*Uweh!*' Epossi went on exclaiming, pinning the backs of her hands on her hips. 'No wonder I saw Auntie Ngea looking so sad when she was passing outside my house.'

'It was she who brought the news,' Ngoso said.

'*Uweh!*' Epossi said and clapped her hands and then pinned them again on her hips.

'They say I killed her.'

'Let them go away with their witchcraft,' Epossi said. 'Having killed her themselves they come and heap the blame on you. Aren't they ashamed?'

'Oh,' he said, 'they say it was because I beat her. She miscarried when she got to Bomono.'

Epossi wasn't convinced. She had once been married to a Pongo man who died three years later. He hadn't even been ill.

So she thought she knew them well. They were full of witchcraft. But that was exactly what Pongos thought of Mongos.

Because you beat her, she thought, as if you are the first man to have beaten a woman.

Ewudu wasn't so indulgent in her interpretation of the accusation. She was horrified although she was used to that kind of treatment herself, those rough beatings! It was the miscarriage part of the story which she found particularly mortifying. So she was leaving Ekema for another wild man?

'Don't worry,' he said to her. 'I can see fear sitting on your face. I won't beat you.'

'But will you still take her with you?'

'Why not?'

'Won't you go to the funeral?'

'She's been buried.'

'But you must go and see her mother.'

'I'll go,' he said, faced with the problem of timing.

There was no point his hurrying to Bomono. The woman had been right. He wouldn't resurrect her. And then maybe something would happen to him if he went; so he could just as well enjoy himself for a few days before going to hear the nonsense which was waiting for him.

Yes, he would go up with Ewudu, stay with her on the farm for about a week, even more and then he would go to Bomono.

'A-Ngoso,' he heard Makole's voice.

He turned round and saw his friend looking very happy as he was paddling softly down the creek.

'How?' he said. 'Have you arrived?'

'Yes,' Makole said; 'Inon has had her baby.'

'Good news,' Ngoso said. 'Boy or girl?'

'She gave birth to Ngos'a Makole,' his friend said expecting Ngoso would jump up with joy because the boy had been named after him.

88

Ngoso was touched by Makole's friendly gesture, especially as it came at a time when Njale had just gone to the grave with the foetus of his own child.

'That is good,' he said to his friend, 'Inon gave me a name-sake. That is very good. When did she deliver?'

'This morning.'

'*A*-Makole,' Epossi said, 'Njale is dead.'

'No!'

'That is what you met us discussing.'

Ngoso turned towards his canoe and took a bunch of plantains which he put in the tray Ewudu had brought. Then he put one bunch across Epossi's little basin. He lifted the tray to Ewudu's head; and Epossi bent down, almost stooping, and lifted her basin to her head.

'*A*-Makole, later,' she said, straightening up.

'No,' Makole said. 'I don't think I'll come to the town. I'll buy a few things and go back.'

'So greet Inon for me.'

'*O*.'

'Ewudu,' Ngoso said. 'Come back as soon as you leave the plantains in the house. Do you hear?'

'Yes.'

'We shall need a few things: fish, oil, kerosene, and a few other things.'

'*O*.'

The two women turned away and began to climb the hill. They soon disappeared in the crowd.

'What really happened?' Makole asked when, having found a place for his canoe, he came over to where Ngoso was selling plantains. He had just sold a bunch to a woman who carried it on her head and went into the market.

'Leave me,' Ngoso said, 'it was Ngea who brought the news.'

They discussed for some time and then Makole who hadn't

brought any plantains to sell went into the market and still Ewudu hadn't returned.

Ngoso sold three more bunches of plantains; then he sold two more; and then three more and still Ewudu hadn't returned from the town. He sold his last bunch and Makole, carrying his paddle and a travelling bag, came out of the market.

'When are you going up?' he asked his friend.

'I don't know,' Ngoso replied, looking terribly bored. 'I would have loved to paddle out with the tide, but I can't.'

'Why not? You have finished selling the plantains. Or are you waiting for Ewudu? I heard you saying to her that she should come and buy a few things. Are you thinking of going up with her?'

'Yes,' Ngoso said smiling in spite of himself.

'Even after the news about Njale?'

Makole put down the bag. The tail fins of a fish could be seen over the brim. It was dried *se*.

'Yes, *a*-Makole,' Ngoso said. 'I had promised to take her with me before I heard the news. Now I can't leave her.'

Makole shrugged his shoulders and picked up his bag.

As he was going to his canoe, he felt very worried about Ngoso. With Njale now dead when would he ever marry again? He used to say he would marry only a woman who was expecting his child. And Njale who had satisfied that condition had gone and died. What kind of misfortune was that? Makole wondered, putting the bag in his canoe.

The wind tossed the branches of the mangrove trees, turning their leaves. Swift birds crossed overhead and on the dark mud of the waterfront butterflies moved their wings like accordions.

After Makole had paddled out of the creek and Ewudu still hadn't returned from the town, Ngoso sat down on the prow of his canoe and looking infront of him, he saw Njale in the depth of his thoughts — her stout body, the large breasts, her long face;

90

the night Dikodu had told the story about the two women! How their man had sent the ugly one away even though she had had a son by him.

Njale!

Ngoso recalled how sad she had looked that night; and how clear the sky had been with its stars! And he recalled noticing the constellation *Bana ba ńuwe*, the orphans, tiny stars grouped together, looking helpless, forlon and destitute. And he had thought of his child when it would be born and of his own death and of Njale's. And he had tried to imagine his son as an orhpan, Mbed'a Ngoso, living on without his parents, something of the past gone forever. An orphan in the face of the future. And he heard his father's voice announcing his mother's death.

'Ngoso,' his father had said sadly that afternoon years ago when Ngoso returned from the river having heard the shrill weep-ing of his step-aunt Longele. 'Ngoso, your mother has gone away.'

He had been fishing in the river and as soon as he heard Longele's voice he knew his mother had died. He hadn't shed any tears until he got home and saw his father and heard the sadness in his voice.

And then two years later, their father died.

How sad he had been, even sadder than his brother Mbongo!

It had been a terrible blow, coming as it did so soon after their mother's death.

The full moon had worn a halo for their father, a sign of the man's greatness, and Ngoso had remained sad for a long time.

Oh his son, an orphan?

No, *a*-death in so many tides, he had thought that night. You are like a flood that uproots some riverside trees while others remain standing spared for a few more days by the fatal erosion. *A*-death, let us bring up our child before you come; death, right to where parrots build their nests and lay their eggs. Death, not before our child becomes a man.

91

And then he had sighed and his thoughts had flowed back to the story-teller's voice; but only for a while.

His child an orphan!

The sky had been very high and in the audience so much compassionate sighing and the old man had talked and talked.

And then that shooting star like a dew-drop reflecting the sun's rays from the other side of the night and the dawn!

He and Njale had returned to their canoe long after the first crowing of the cocks and *Tole*, the morning star, was already shining.

15

Anger provoked by Ewudu's delay took the place of sadness and memories in his thoughts as he rose and went to the town. But before going to the house where she had spent the night he decided he would drink a cup or two of palmwine. Something must have happened, he thought.

And then he told himself that let it happen. What else could be more than Njale's death? He would put a little palmwine in his system and then he would go and find out the meaning of that kind of behaviour.

A few people were on the verandah of the palmwine seller's hut, drinking and conversing, some looking very alert and gay, others drowsy and morose.

He greeted them. Some answered in a warm chorus while

others only hummed, their heads drooping, chins resting against their chests, their aspect bored.

Ngoso sat down.

'A cup of palmwine,' he said.

'I haven't cups,' the palmwine seller, a corpulent man with a round face, said. He had just opened his business. His hut was new, the thatches fresh as was the earthen floor of the verandah. 'Shall I serve you a glass?' he asked Ngoso.

'Yes.'

The corpulent man filled up a glass for him. Ngoso took the drink and tasted it. He didn't think the wine was as good as Malende's. He thought it was a bit diluted. But maybe it wasn't the seller's fault. He must have bought it like that; after all he wasn't a tapper himself.

Ngoso emptied the glass and held it to the trader who filled it up.

Yes, he thought, Njale is dead. Yes, my child as well. Who knows whether it would have been a boy? Oh, why did I beat her? Why? I shall never beat a woman again in my life. But why didn't Ewudu come back?

That headache again! And he thought he was going to be feverish. Recently he was often feverish. But why should I be feverish again?

He drank half the glass and when he looked up he saw Ewudu passing. She was with a hefty man who was dressed in a cheap suit, a man he had never seen before.

'Ewudu!' he called.

The people who were with him on the verandah looked towards the street. The man who was with Ewudu looked back; but she tugged at his arm impatiently and they continued on their way.

Ngoso emptied his glass of wine and put it down by his right foot. So she was now afraid of him?

The other customers exchanged looks; and some looked at Ngoso with the irony-charged expression of they-have-taken-her-from-you in their hazy eyes.

But a wind soon moved up the street, raising dust and bits of paper and dry leaves which danced briefly, spiralling in the air. This wind seemed to blow the irony and the whole matter from everybody's mind save Ngoso's. He would see the end of that kind of behaviour, he swore in his thoughts.

The palmwine seller and his customers resumed their merry, though strangely sober conversation — at least those of them who had the vein for merry-talk. Those who were very drunk were silent, thinking, or maybe not thinking at all.

Ewudu and her companion had disappeared behind the dust raised by the whirlwind; and when the dust cleared they were gone.

Ngoso drank two more glasses of palmwine and then he began to feel more and more indignant. He was sure she had seen him. Or, even if she hadn't seen him, she must certainly have heard him, and recognised his voice. Then why had she ignored him?

How could she? A woman who, as they were leaving the stall last night, had said he had left her waist, hips and thighs with the seams off!

And now because she was walking with a man in an old suit she couldn't even stop to talk to him!

In his imagination he saw the expression of pride, anger and scorn which had been on the man's face.

He had actually seen the face only briefly; but its features remained in his mind. It was a small face for one so hefty. The cheek bones were high. The mouth was small with the lower lip shorter than the upper lip. He had a mark on the right cheek such as some Bakweris have. He looked very pompous and he was much taller than Ngoso who also noticed that his rival — for

94

that was what he already was to him — looked a very determined man.

And I had waited for her on the waterfront, he thought; and then his imagination became prospective. If Ewudu too would die then let her die. He would teach her. Who ever told her that?

Then something occurred to him when he recalled the mark on the man's cheek. Could he be Ewudu's lover?

He ordered another glass of palmwine. He was drinking it when a strange melancholy came over him. It was a kind of beautiful sadness, a kind of subtle despair. He felt as if he hadn't a brother and a step-aunt whom he loved and who loved him; as if he hadn't friends and a sprinkling of lovers and relatives in Mongo and elsewhere. He felt alone.

The sun will rise over Mungo River, he thought, and I will be there, alone, like a widower, without a woman, without children. And the sun will set over me and my farm.

No; that I'll go up today, get home, make myself something to throw into my belly and then go to bed and wait for sleep and for patridges to announce the dawn without a woman in my bed?

That won't be right. I must get married and I have chosen Ewudu. We shall see.

He emptied his glass, paid the palmwine seller and went to Epossi's place.

'Where's Ewudu?' he asked the woman.

'Sit down,' she said. 'That's your food. It's Ewudu who prepared it for you. Sit down and eat.'

'Where's she herself?'

'She's gone.'

'Where?'

'To the camp.'

'With the man in a suit?'

'You saw them?'

'Yes,' he said. 'I said again that that must be that Bakweriman.'

'You missed something.'

'What did he say?'

'Are you asking me? I Eposs'a Mukole mu Mwanja who didn't go to their schools, what could I have made of all the books he poured out there?'

'But Ewudu didn't tell me that he was going to come and meet her in Mudeka.'

'It looks as though he decided it would be better for him to come and meet her so that they might return to the camp together. And then to have arrived only to hear about you.'

'Who do you think told him?'

'You are even asking. Why do you think Esadi has that large mouth? She must have told Ekema that they were sleeping with his woman all over Mudeka and that if he wasn't careful he would lose her.'

Ngoso recalled how last night Esadi had said her sister was an animal just because she had allowed him to make love to her.

Who knew whether Ekema had turned up only because he had received word from Esadi about Ewudu? But Ngoso didn't care. His mind was made up.

Epossi looked behind her and satisfied with the position of a bokuka stool which stood by the door, she lowered herself on it and looked at the street outside.

People went in both directions, those returning from the market and those who were going towards it. Bicycles, their bells ringing. That was all one could see in Mudeka those days. No cars. No lorries. One had to leave the town and enter the rubber plantation where Ewudu's man worked for one to see a narrow gauge railway which linked the plantations with Tiko and the wharf. And sometimes one saw carriages drawn by a diesel engine, or simply a push or pump trolley. Locomotives used the Mondoni-Tiko line. Some came to Missellele. But only diesel engines came to fetch the rubber tapped in the plantations near Mudeka.

'Eat,' the woman said, turning her eyes from the street to look at Ngoso who was still standing in the centre of the parlour. 'She said she'd cook a little something for you before going back to the market to buy the things you said. The food was still on the fire when her man entered like a bad storm. It was I who finished cooking the food. He wouldn't even wait until the food was ready so that she might put a little something in her belly. He took her to the market and then I was standing in this door when I saw them passing. Sit down and eat.'

'*Na*,' he said, sitting down at the table where only last night they had discussed his plans about her. 'That's one person. Njale is dead. Ewudu is gone.'

'*Mba ma*,' she said sympathetically and turned her look outside.

He sat back, raised his loin-cloth and put his hand into the pocket of the pair of shorts he wore under the loin-cloth.

'Take,' he said.

'What?'

He counted some cash from his right hand into the palm of his left hand. He put back some money in his pocket. And then returning the rest into his right hand, he gave it to her.

'Take my bag,' he said. 'Take out the machete and my old hat. There are bottles in it. Take them to the market and buy me some palm oil and kerosene. Be careful how you put back the bottles in the bag and have them well-corked; and be careful about which one is for kerosene and which one is for oil. Also buy me a dried *se*. Then buy three towels and four small singlets for Inon's child.'

16

She waited for him to finish eating. Then when he had left for the camp she went to the market, fearing he would get himself into trouble.

Ngoso still remembered the number of Ewudu's friend's room and as soon as he got to the camp which was about an hour's walk from Mudeka, he went there only to find a padlock on the door. He shrugged his shoulders and decided to go to the other end of the camp where people were singing. They must be drinking corn beer.

Someone swore aloud. There was laughter and more drunken swearing. And two people began to sing so loud that you thought they were going to sing out their throats, as if they wanted to do all the singing of a lifetime that day.

"Afternoon,' he said when he got to the other end of the camp and looked into the room where people were drinking corn beer.

The two people weren't singing anymore. Maybe they had broken into song while they were leaving the place and they were now somewhere else, in another part of the camp, or they were under the rubber trees, going to Missellele or to another camp. It was Sunday and workers enjoyed themselves.

Hard work would resume the following day—rubber-tapping and clearing of the plantation. They would all be dressed in rags with the exception of the women who didn't work on the plantation. Some women worked in hospitals and offices in places like Tiko, Missellele, Bota and Ekona; but here, where most of the work was manual only the men did it, wearing rags.

But today they were dressed in fine shirts and large loin-cloths, trousers, pairs of shorts, and a few even wore suits like the one Ewudu's lover had been wearing earlier that afternoon.

"Afternoon,' some of them replied, including of course the woman who sold the corn beer. She was fat.

'How?' she added, revealing uneven teeth. '*You came here?*'

'Yes,' Ngoso said, going in.

The woman pushed a stool towards him and asked him if he wouldn't sit down.

The room was smoky. Ngoso sat down; he ordered a drink. His rival wasn't there and Ewudu was somewhere in the camp. What was she thinking that very moment? What was she doing? He felt very sad again and very lonely.

A guitarist was strumming away, singing in a series of staccato moans, his head leaning against the wall, his eyes half-closed, a cigarette at the corner of his mouth. He was accompanied by a fellow who made music on an empty bottle, hitting it rhythmically with a nickel spoon.

And Ngoso sat there, drinking until darkness fell outside and his head began to droop, a pointless smile on his ruddy face and soon he was feeling sleepy.

Someone lit a lantern. Maybe it was the fat woman. Ngoso couldn't say. All he knew was that a lamp was now standing before him. It was night. The lantern was on the floor. And he was perspiring, especially on his hairy chest and under his armpits.

The guitarist was still playing, still moaning melodiously as if in a dream to the accompaniment of the bottle.

Smiling and frowning and swaying Ngoso got up and then he remembered he hadn't paid for the beer he had drunk. He put his hand in his pocket, brought out money and paid the woman and went out.

'Ko, ko, ko,' he soon found himself saying at the door of Ewudu's friend's room.

99

'Who is that?'

'A man,' he said, swaying and smiling.

He pushed open the door and a woman came out from behind a curtain which divided the room into two, thus hiding the bed.

'What's the matter?' she asked.

He put a finger on his lips, asking her to be silent. Then he asked, 'Your man, is he in?'

'No,' she said.

She was as small as Ewudu. Ngoso smiled some more and swayed even though he had his hands on either side of the door-frame.

'Ewudu,' he said. 'You know her?'

'Yes,' she said and understood. Ekema had talked and talked about him that afternoon, fuming. So this was the 'bushman'? He was an imposing man, she thought, look at his broad chest! 'Come in,' she said.

'Go and tell Ewudu that her man has arrived,' he said, going in.

The woman drew up a chair for him by a table on which a lamp stood. An old gramophone was also on the table.

He slumped into the chair, folded his arms on the table and leaned his head against them, closing his eyes.

'Go and tell her that I am going back with her this night,' he added, feeling sleepy.

Because he had spent the night in the canoe he hadn't been able to sleep. Now, he would rest a bit before returning to Mudeka; and he would be paddling all night to return to his farm.

When he opened his eyes later it was because he had heard the woman calling him:

'*Sango, sango, sango.*'

She put her hand on his shoulder and he sighed deeply; then he sat up, realising that he had been sleeping for quite a while.

He was very glad about that; and he felt it was time for them to leave.

'Ewudu?' he said, looking at the woman.

'She's coming,' she said. 'Take the cup and wash your face. That's the food she sent. Get up and wash your face and eat.'

He wasn't smiling anymore. He frowned, scratching his face with the tips of his fingers, then he put his hand inside his shirt and scratched his big chest.

'Did I sleep?' he asked, his mouth feeling stale.

'Yes,' she said. 'You slept like a log. Ewudu has even been here; but she said I shouldn't wake you up.'

'Why?'

'She said she wanted you to rest for a while.'

'Is her man there?'

'Yes,' she said, sitting on the bed with the curtain behind her.

He took the cup of water to the verandah, washed his face and flushed his mouth. He went back to the room and sat down.

'Is she coming,' he asked, opening one of the two dishes the woman had set for him on the table.

'Yes.'

She came, carrying two travelling bags.

'Didn't he see you?' her friend asked.

'No,' Ewudu said, looking worried and uncertain, feeling unsafe.

'Wasn't he in the house?' her friend added.

'He was sitting on the verandah. I left him there. Ngoso, let's go.'

'And the bags,' the other woman asked.

'Ugh!' Ewudu cried. 'How inquisitive you are? While he was outside I dumped my things in the bag and passed it through the window. Then the other bag. After all it was already packed. I hadn't touched it since we returned from Mudeka.'

'You are something,' her friend said in admiration.

'So I also lowered it outside the window. And then I passed him and went round the house and picked up my bags. He's sitting outside his door. Ngoso, let's go.'

They got to Mudeka.

'You brought her?' Epossi asked when Ngoso knocked at her door.

'All day,' he said proudly.

'Your lie!'

'Open the door,' Ewudu said.

'*Uweh!*' Epossi exclaimed '*A*-Ngoso!'

'My bag,' he said when she opened the door.

They went in.

'Ewudu!' the woman with a long neck and large breasts cried, clapping her hands. '*A*-Ngoso! No; you shouldn't have done that to Ekema, poor him! How did you manage it?'

'I say my bag,' he said.

She went into the room and returned with his bag and paddle.

'How did you do it?' she asked, surprised, pleased. But she was also worried even though she didn't want to realise it. She knew Ekema would react. How could she say what he would do?

'Ewudu,' she insisted, 'you tell me.'

'We shall tell you about it some other time,' Ngoso said, taking his paddle and the bag. 'Was the money enough?'

'Yes,' she said. 'Some of it remained.'

'Keep it for yourself,' he said. 'You know I am a rich man.' He meant it as a joke.

'That's right,' she said. 'Now that you've snatched a woman from a Bakweriman one wouldn't hear any other thing. Look at his face!'

He smiled, glancing at Ewudu who was looking very tired and afraid.

'Let's go,' she said. 'If he meets us here?'

'What can he do?' he asked.

'Shut up,' Epossi said. 'Do you know Ekema?'

'Leave him,' Ewudu said, fearing the mere thought of what Ekema might do. Who knew if he wasn't already on the way? 'I say let's go,' she repeated. She was all impatience and anxiety. 'Ngoso, let's go.'

Somehow she began to feel that even when they got to his farm she wouldn't feel better, she wouldn't feel any more secure.

'Epossi,' he said, suddenly looking distracted.

He had won; but he still had to make his victory permanent; he still had to make it part of his tomorrow. Even to him that didn't seem easy. Maybe using the same cleverness as she had shown that night she would run away from him one day. And with that thought he felt what Ekema must have been feeling that very moment and he knew the man wouldn't forgive him. Ekema's honour was involved in this and he recalled the things Ewudu had said about his mother.

'Yes?'

Ngoso put his hand on his forehead. 'I've even forgotten what I wanted to say,' he said. 'Yes, a mat.'

'What do you want to do with a mat?'

'It's for Ewudu. I'll spread it for her in the canoe. She'll need some sleep.'

'If those mosquitoes would let me sleep,' she said, feeling better and very young.

He was strong and kind. That was good. He was the kind of man she liked — at least that was what she thought. She seemed to have forgotten about what she had heard that morning. She didn't want to think of it. So it was as if she had forgotten everything about Njale.

Later, as they were leaving Mudeka, he wasn't sure whether or not he had done the right thing. Njale had almost been his wife. He wished he had thought of it earlier. He would have bought a few things for her mother. Black cloth for her mourning and some tobacco for her pipe.

While he was paddling and thinking of the trip he would make to Njale's people, Ewudu was trying to sleep, lying on planks over which he had spread the mat he had borrowed from Epossi. But the mosquitoes wouldn't let her have the least peace as if they had been sent by Ekema. They sang to her songs she didn't want to hear and they pinched her as if to remind her of things about which she didn't want to think. And he paddled and paddled, imagining she was sleeping.

'Ewudu,' he said when they got to Mongo after he had paddled from one creek to another until he joined the Mungo river itself with its banks which were flanked by huge raffia palms. 'Ewudu, we are in Mongo.'

'Already?' she asked, sitting up.

'I thought you were sleeping.'

'Where? The useless mosquitoes wouldn't let me. You want to call?'

'To do what?'

'Well, I don't know.'

A cock crew.

'Is that the first cock or the second?'

'I think it's the first,' he said, 'the day is still far away.'

'Our good fortune that we are passing in the night,' she observed. 'What wouldn't they have said? Especially after hearing about Njale. I am sure the news has reached here. And then knowing that Mbongo is with Ndutu' — her sister — 'aye, they would have killed us with their mouthiness.'

'Good fortune is on us,' he said. 'I had begun to wonder how I could ever leave that camp without you.'

'I say!' she said. 'Ekema will kill himself. What? To go into the room and discover that I had packed all my things while he was sitting on the verandah!'

'At first I thought it was the tide,' he said because he didn't want to think of her as a scheming woman, 'but it looks as though the water has come.'

'You think so?'

He didn't reply. The beaches were all calm, very dark under their huge mango trees. The water made a gurgling sound against the reeds and Ngoso noticed the level of the water was really high.

'Yes,' he said. 'The water has come. See how covered the north is.'

He looked back. The sky was lightly clouded and it seemed already touched by the clarity of dawn. He turned his look in front, paddling softly.

'The north is full of clouds,' she said.

But he didn't say anything.

The north towards which he was paddling was indeed heavily clouded. It was as if the sky-high clouds were growing on the riverbanks. After a bend or two up the river there seemed to be no trees. Only clouds and they were very dark.

'I regret having left my basin in his place,' she said because she was frightened by their silence. 'And his new bag which I took.' Still he didn't say anything. 'A-Ngoso,' she said, 'aren't you hearing?'

'What?'

'No,' she said. 'I was just wondering about Ekema.'

'Forget him,' he said.

'Ngoso, I don't know,' she said vaguely, sighing. 'When I think of his mother — '

'If you haven't something else to talk about then keep quiet.'

'But, Ngoso.'

'But, Ngoso, what? Where you born for him?'

'I didn't say so,' she admitted for no one was born for any one person in particular. People were born free. They could choose their partners — if not always their husbands and wives, at least those to whom they gave themselves in sécret behind the back of the night and the day. That was what she had done since she became a woman; that was what she was now doing, giving herself to him for as long as life would allow it.

'What then did you say?' he asked.

'Now what has annoyed you?'

In the silence which soon intervened between them, she desired him desperately and she wished the canoe would go faster without his having to paddle it because she didn't want him to tire himself out.

I7

By the time he was paddling into his beach he had decided he wouldn't rush to Bomono since, judging from what the woman had said, his presence there wouldn't be particularly appreciated; in fact it might even be interpreted as a kind of provocation. He would therefore spend about a week with Ewudu on the farm; and then he would leave her with Makole's wife and then he would go away for two days or three.

As the prow of the canoe touched the soft earth, Ewudu took hold of a post to which he chained his canoe.

She disembarked.

From the helm he went to the prow and passed her the bags, one after the other. She put them down. Then, the canoe swaying, almost as he had been swaying in the camp after the cornbeer, he stalked back to the helm, and fetched his paddle and machete which he had removed from his bag and had kept near him so that he could use it on any snake which might drop into the canoe from the branches which hung over the riverbanks. Snakes sometimes dropped into canoes, long snakes and while the woman or women in the canoe screamed, the canoeman attacked it with his machete, cut it and using the machete, scraped it into the river.

'So this is home,' he said as he was chaining the canoe.

'Home,' she said doubtfully.

'Yes,' he said, surprised at the doubt in her voice.

'A,' she said. 'Why don't you live in Mongo and come from there to the farm?'

He put his machete upside down in the travelling bag which had the fish, the oil and the kerosene he had asked Epossi to buy for him, as well as the towels and singlets for Makole's son.

His paddle was in his left hand and with the right he picked up one of Ewudu's bags and then with the hand which had the paddle he took his own bag.

'Take the other bag,' he said.

They began to climb the steep bank. She walked ahead of him.

'I can't understand how one can live all alone here like this,' she said.

'That is why I brought you,' he said.

'You think I'll be able to stand it?'

'Why not? Didn't you live in Njopongo?'

'Did they tell you that I liked it there? And please don't remind me of Njopongo.'

That was because the aunt with whom she had been living there had died.

'You'll like it here,' he said, hating the idea of his ever having to leave the farm to go and live in Mongo. That farm was his life. What he needed was a lot of children to make the place noisy and lively. There could be no question of his going to live in Mongo and then only coming from there to work on the farm.

'Yes,' he said.

When they got to his compound he looked back at the lovely river. It had become wider, more muscular.

River of legends about mermaids and other water creatures. Legends and stories about mysterious craft — very long race canoes manned by ghosts, legends about launches and even ships — and big water snakes which were said to span the river sometimes at night, from bank to bank, to block the way against a bewitched canoeman.

Innocent canoemen only had to declare their lineage, reciting with reverence and with pride the great names of their genealogy and beating their chests and saying such a thing could never happen to them on that river, their river.

Never. And the snake shortened itself, as if in deference, leaving one bank clear for the canoe to pass after which the snake blocked the river again, waiting for the next canoeman to challenge its mission and lay claim to the right to peaceful passage.

Ewudu put down the bag outside the hut and sighed. She was very tired and sleepy.

He passed her and went to the verandah, put the bags down and leaned his paddle against the thatched wall.

He opened the door and groped towards the table on which he had left his lantern two days ago. His hand touched the old table on which a bucket of river-water stood. Then his hand touched the lantern. A dish and a plate out of which he had eaten before setting out for Mudeka was also on the table.

He put his hand into the breast pocket of his shirt and took out a handkerchief; then a packet of cigarettes which had only five or four cigarettes left.

'Ugh,' he said, angry with himself. 'I forgot to buy cigarettes!'

'Uweh!' she said. 'But why did you forget again to buy cigarettes?'

He struck a match and lit the lamp and Ewudu came in with her bag; then she brought in the other bags. And then she sat down by the table.

He went out and brought in his paddle and took it to his sleeping room.

Outside the overcast dawn seemed to be breathing. A soft humming sound came from the river.

He was attached to the farm, here where his parents were buried. and he was attached to the river.

He feared it would be a very sad rainy season. He didn't know why he was feeling like that.

He returned to the parlour and then went out into the darkness and walked towards the river; but he soon branched off to his left and walked into the much thicker darkness under the cocoa trees. But where was he going?

Two bends down the path stood the little grave yard. He now thought of it once more and wished he had some strong drink in the house for a libation.

Yes, he would have liked to talk to his parents and his uncle about Ewudu. They too must have heard about his other woman. They must have heard of her if the dead ever hear which he hoped they did.

'I want children,' he said aloud in the darkness, but not too loud, knowing it was a wish his parents, especially his mother, would sympathise with.

He went back to the hut. He met Ewudu staring before her, her thoughts wandering in space.

What was she thinking about, he wondered; then he hoped in his feelings that she was seeing all her future days and his united, flanked by countless mornings and nights.

He sat down by the table on which he put his left arm.

'What is that?' she asked a few moments later, listening, a thoughtful frown on her face and she was looking slightly older.

Ngoso listened. 'Rain,' he said, as the drops increased on the thatched roof.

The hut was soon surrounded by what sounded like a storm. The rain was heavy and fierce.

'I'm going to sleep,' he said after a short silence.

He rose, undid his loin-cloth and then threw it about him.

Ewudu also rose and taking the lantern they went into the sleeping room.

It rained heavily throughout the dawn and in her sleep she dreamt of the rain.

And in the morning when she woke up it was still raining.

In the depth of his sleep he sensed that she had woken up and so he stirred, bent double, stretched himself and yawned:

A-Mbed'a Bonam!'

He turned and lay on his side, facing her.

'Are you up?' she asked.

'Yes,' he replied. 'How did you sleep?'

'Well,' she said and put her arm on his side. 'And you?'

'Well.'

They remained in bed until the rain stopped towards noon and the sun arose.

Then he went out. The wetness which the rain had left on the leaves and on the ground was rising in a fine vapour.

Birds flew about, singing, from branch to branch, from plantain leaves to the grasses on the edge of the land.

On his right one of his hens was scratching into the dark

110

earth. He heard footfalls and presently a man emerged from the grassy footpath which ran along the river.

''Morning,' he greeted Ngoso.

''Morning,' Ngoso replied.

The traveller hurried on his way, entering the cocoa trees. He had a stave on his shoulder. A straw bag hung from the stave, resting against his back.

The river had risen very high and the water was muddy. It looked tacky and reluctant flowing towards the ocean in the south.

'He decided to shift the moorings of his canoe; so he went to the beach where he took off his loin-cloth, folded it carefully and put it on a log from the top of which the rain had evaporated.

His canoe was now under the water.

He went into the river. The water felt cold. That was when he thought of the key. Let it be, he thought; he wouldn't go back for it. He took hold of the canoe and brought it to the surface and then he began to push it, first to the right and then to the left, right left, right left and each time some of the water in it splashed out and then he began to shake it, pressing the side he was holding down and then letting it roll up again and all the time more water splashed out of the canoe; right left, right left, up down, up down, right left, right left, up down, until very little water remained in the canoe.

Now he waded out of the water and took the post to which he had chained the canoe the previous night in his two hands, shook it and then removed it from the ground.

He walked a few paces up the hill and pinned the post into the ground where he was sure the water wouldn't reach that day.

After that he took his tooth stick from his mouth and put it carefully on his loin-cloth.

The sunshine was very dull.

He jumped into the water, swam out, northwards, and then back to the beach.

A canoe loaded with plantains appeared from the bend upstream. The canoeman's paddle was in the water; but he wasn't paddling. He let the current carry the canoe. Maybe he was going to Duala or to Tiko.

A woman was in the middle of the canoe. She was bailing out water, using a *mboso*. She bailed the water noisily, the mboso scraping the side of the canoe and the water she bailed out splashing on the river.

The canoe was so loaded that only about two inches of its sides were above the water. The canoeman was talking to the woman, his wife perhaps or only a lover.

Ngoso swam out again, cutting the water with deft strokes of his arms, his feet propelling him forward; sometimes he took water in his mouth, deliberately, then he spat it out, throwing his head this side and that.

He didn't know the people in the canoe and they didn't know him. If they had been acquaintances they would have raised their voices to exchange greetings and bits of news with him. But he didn't know them.

Later that afternoon, he and Ewudu went to Makole's place up the river.

'Inon!' he shouted as soon as they got ashore. 'I've come to see my namesake's face. Is he as ugly as you?'

'*Wo!*' Makole's sister-in-law said from the hut. 'Ngoso has come.' She appeared in the doorway. 'But who again am I seeing with him like that? Ewudu!'

'Inon!' Ngoso called.

They got to the hut.

'How?' he asked Makole's sister-in-law. 'Are you well?'

'Not as much as you,' she said, looking at him from the corner of her eye; then she turned towards Ewudu whose hand she shook. 'Have you come here?' she asked coldly.

'Yes,' Ewudu replied, slightly embarrassed.

Ngoso went in, followed by Ewudu and then he asked where Makole's wife was.

'In the room,' Inon's sister said.

Ngoso and Ewudu went into the room where a log fire was burning not far from the bed on which Inon was fast asleep, her long and full breasts naked, her beautiful, oiled face reflecting the log fire.

Her child was in a basin by the bedside, a charming baby swaddled in towels, holding his tiny fists clenched.

Ngoso bent forward, his face over the basin which served as a cot.

It was very warm in the room.

'It's altogether Makole,' Ngoso said, seeing his friend's receding forehead in the baby's face and in the virtually hairless head the meagerness of hair which was noticeable in Makole who had never grown what could be called a beard. He wasn't like Ngoso who had to shave often.

'Look at his bald head,' Ngoso said.

'It's not true,' Inon's sister said. 'Look at his head properly and you'll see that he came out with his own few hairs.'

'I have seen,' Ngoso said.

'And you see how handsome he is?' Makole's sister-in-law said, 'like his father.'

'I say I have seen,' Ngoso said, 'but he's a bit bald.'

Makole's sister-in-law looked at him from the corner of her eye.

'Although his father hasn't a forest such as the one you have here,' she said, gripping Ngoso's overgrown hair, 'did they tell you that he is bald?'

'*Aye*,' Ngoso said, 'altogether Makole's face.' Then, turning towards Makole's wife, he shouted: '*A*-Inon!'

113

'Don't wake her up,' Ewudu said, bending down to admire the child more closely. She loved children.

'*Diba*,' he barked at her. 'Shut up.' He smiled at the sleeping woman. '*E-e*,' he said, 'look at her face.'

Inon breathed in deeply, then she breathed out; then she stirred; and, opening her eyes, she smiled.

'*A*-Ngoso,' she said sleepily, 'have you come?'

'*E-e*,' he said, 'look at her.'

'Go away,' Inon said, smiling, dimples forming on her cheeks.

'But you look at whom he has brought,' her sister said. 'Ewudu.'

Inon looked towards the basin in which the child was. Of course from the time she had opened her eyes she saw the woman who was with him; but she hadn't thought that was Ewudu. When her husband had returned from the market the previous evening, he hadn't told them anything about her. He hadn't said Ngoso would be coming up with her.

'Ewudu,' she said.

'*E*,' Ewudu said.

'Is that how you have grown up?' The room was very warm. The brands sparked in the fire; and beyond the roof parrots returning from the sao trees in Missaka whistled noisily, crying and laughing and saying, it seemed, that they would return again to the fruit trees before night-fall, the night which would oblige them to fly back to their far-away nests.

'I didn't recognise you,' Inon added.

'But why are you still carrying that bag?' Ngoso asked Ewudu.

It wasn't her fault. Inon's sister hadn't offered to relieve her of it. Ewudu now held it to her.

'What is in it?' she asked, taking the bag.

'Things Ngoso bought for the child,' Ewudu said, 'and some fish.'

Inon smiled without joy for she was thinking of Ngoso's child. She felt touched that in spite of everything there he was bringing presents to her son when his was dead with its mother.

She recalled the day they had discussed Njale and Ngoso had said she was his eye. He had been very proud of himself when he had alluded to her pregnancy.

Inon was remembering all that now. A terrible thing, she thought, wondering how to introduce Njale into their conversation; how to talk about the news her husband had brought from the market yesterday, how to talk about it without having to remind Ngoso that Njale had been pregnant.

No, I'll have to tell him. He shouldn't have done it — to bring another woman to her bed immediately after what has just happened. That is not right at all.

The painful, pensive smile left her face and its place was taken by a thoughtful frown. It made her look much older. For the first time Ngoso felt towards her the same feeling he had for his step-aunt in Bojongo. Profound love and respect.

From outside came the mournful cry of a hornbill lamenting the dry season and accepting as a compensation the delicious *sao* of the rainy season, tasty fruit. The hornbill complaining of the wetness of the season and of the leaves and branches. For how long, he seemed to be asking, for how long: howng-ho, howng-ho! Although traditionally he was said to be looking for *kang*, a fellow bird, who was supposed to have robbed the hornbill of his original plumage, the beautiful spotted plumage which Kang was now wearing.

'But where is Makole himself,' Ngoso asked.

'He's gone to load firewood in the canoe,' Inon's sister said, taking the bag to the other room where she emptied it.

'Firewood?'

'Yes. He's going down to Duala tomorrow morning ... A-Ngoso.'

'Yes?'

'Ngoso,' Inon said, turning to lie on her back, her eyes turned towards the roof from which mazes of spider's web made brown by smoke hung, stirred by the breadth of the fire. 'I won't hide it from you,' she said. 'I'm not happy with you.'

'Is it about Njale?'

'Yes.'

'Inon, I know.'

'Yes,' she mused, not looking at him. 'It's not right at all.'

Now she turned to face him; she stretched her hand towards her child and fidgeted with the towels in the basin not because they needed arranging but simply out of tenderness.

Yes, he thought once more; the child is his father himself.

He used to think of Makole as 'a drop of a man,' because his friend was small in stature. Looking at the child Ngoso felt he too would be like his father, a little serious-looking, and occasionally very rascally man.

When Makole returned about an hour or so later, Njale was discussed again, more fully, in an atmosphere which resembled a family meeting. But the name itself was mentioned sparingly; almost with discretion; and it was decided that Ngoso would leave Ewudu with them while he went to Bomono. He didn't raise the question of the threat to his life because he didn't want to make them begin to worry about his safety.

They had heard the parrots returning to Missaka and soon they would be flying across the river, flying back to their nests and their eggs.

If he hadn't brought Ewudu he would have hurried back to his farm, harvested a few plantains and gone down with Makole the following morning.

And then inexplicably, Ewudu began to cry.

'Ewudu,' Makole's wife asked, 'what's the matter?'

'Nothing,' Ewudu said, rubbing her eyes with the back of her hand and sobbing.

'What is it?'

'Nothing.'

'Then why are you crying?'

Outside it began to drizzle.

'She's like the day,' Makole said. 'She changes. Let her just smile now and you'll see the sun shining outside even though it's almost night.'

Ngoso rose from his chair. 'A-Makole,' he said, 'tomorrow call at my place when you are going down. I'll give you money to buy mourning cloth for her mother, a little tobacco, rice and some salt fish which I'll take to Bomono.'

'All right,' his friend promised. 'But are you going?'

'Yes,' Ngoso said. 'Ewudu, get up.'

'Why don't you wait and eat something?' Inon said.

'No,' Ngoso said. 'When Ewudu is crying like this I have to take her home to pamper her.'

'We've understood,' Makole's sister-in-law said.

'But you can't go in this rain?' Inon said.

'Where's the rain?' Ngoso asked. 'Is it those few drops that you call rain?'

'All right go,' Makole's sister-in-law said.

'Ewudu, let's go,' he said, stepping into the wet dusk.

'Ngoso,' Makole's wife called, 'which day again?'

'Maybe tomorrow,' he said, 'or day after tomorrow.'

'O.'

Cocoa trees lined the slippery road to the beach. You could hear the sound of big isolated drops of rain from the leaves and branches falling on the ground in dismal thuds interspersed with the chirping of insects. The smell of decaying cocoa pods was in the air.

Ngoso's footfalls were solid and firm in spite of the slipperiness of the road. Ewudu walked more delicately for she was small.

18

Makole went to Duala and returned three days later with the black cloth, the rice, fish and tobacco Ngoso had asked him to buy for him, and also with the news that his mother's health was deteriorating. He would be going to Duala again in four days' time.

On the eve of that day Ewudu wept again inexplicably. At least Ngoso could find no explanation for her crying and she didn't give him one. But really she was crying because she was afraid their affair wouldn't last. Her senses felt that the passion they had forged together in the wet warmth of their bodies wouldn't endure the strain of her past and his past; and yet she felt she loved him now even more than she had loved him during the past week; but for how long would he be for her alone? And what would happen to her should she leave him? But leave him for whom? For Ekema?

Then she did something crazy. She went into their room and searched among her things for the two dresses Ekema had bought for her and for the silk headscarf his mother had given her as a present as they were leaving Lysoka.

She found one of the dresses, then the other and the headscarf. She carried them in her hands and went out and Ngoso followed her, not understanding what was happening.

He followed her to the riverside and watched her dump the two dresses and the headscarf into the river; and then she stood back, watching, as the current was carrying them away, and she felt a strange sense of liberation and with it a deepening in intensity of the emotion which held her to Ngoso.

Love; but for how long?

And doubting, she participated in advance in the suffering of departure — the regrets and frustration of the parting of the ways of the heart, the calling off of commitments to yesterday and the days before yesterday. Somehow she felt that soon she might be wearing the shreds of all the protective passion for which, falsely, joy, pleasure and happiness usually predict a very long life.

She didn't know that love was the fear that tenderness always has an end. She didn't know that love was passionate fear on the frontiers of sentimental departure. And so she suffered without knowing why, feeling only that she loved him as she had never loved before.

And yet when Makole called at the farm the following morning Ewudu said she wanted to go to Duala with him since Ngoso would soon be away. She said she liked Makole's wife very much but she didn't think she could ever get on with his sister-in-law; and she didn't want to go to Mongo. It was too near Ekema, just as the farm was by the way.

'Do you know that he only has to cross Mwanda,' she pointed out, 'and he would be on the other side?'

'Then what is he waiting for?' Ngoso asked. 'Let him come. I'll hold his head in the water.'

They all laughed and Ewudu was slightly sorry for Ekema. Somewhere in her heart she tried to side with him because it was too disgraceful that they were laughing at him like that as if he was altogether worthless and they wanted her to be ashamed of him. She found this unfair; so she willed herself towards feeling proud of him. She was doing it for her own pride.

'So you want to go down with Makole?'

'Yes,' she said.

'All right, go and prepare your things.'

They agreed on a certain day he would go to Duala to fetch

her. That would be in seven days' time. He said she should wait for him in the morning in the shop of a certain cloth merchant whom they all knew.

'*A*-Makole,' he said from the beach as the current was carrying his friend's canoe down the river.

'What?' Makole asked, looking back, an old felt hat on his head. And he wore a stained pair of shorts and a torn singlet.

'Paddle well,' Ngoso said, feeling very sentimental. 'You know Ewudu is my life. So be careful the way you paddle that useless canoe of yours.' It was a new canoe. 'Do you hear?'

'Yes,' his friend said and dug the water with his paddle and pulled.

The following afternoon Njale turned up at the farm and Ngoso swore Ewudu was a witch! She had run away in time as if she knew Njale would be coming back.

'*Uweh!*' he cried. 'A ghost has come out of the grave! *A*-Njale! Didn't your aunt Ngea say you were dead?'

'Didn't your aunt Ngea, didn't your aunt Ngea,' she said, putting down the basin she was carrying on her head. 'I never knew that if I should die you would stay seven days without even thinking of coming to see my mother. *A*-Ngoso, aren't you ashamed?'

He was so happy that he couldn't help joking.

'Your aunt told me that if I went they'll kill me.'

'So you didn't know that she said that because she knew that only such a threat would make you want to come?'

'*Uweh!* What a liar Ngea is!'

'Look at his face!'

'*Uweh!*' he exclaimed again, 'if death were to be like this, that I Ngos'a Mbedi would be sitting here on this verandah as I am sitting now and then see that old man,' he meant his late father, 'coming out of that road, saying: "Good, my son. I can see your woman is pregnant." Or Endal'a Bola ... A-Njale!'

'A-Njale!' she said in her coarse voice. 'A week since we've been waiting for you.'

'A week!' he said, 'you think death is something to joke about?'

'Then why didn't you come when you heard that I had died.'

'What a liar that woman Ngea is! And she lies with a serious face!'

She took in the basin and then came back to the verandah.

'Look at him,' she said fondly.

'How is your mother?'

'She's well.'

'Tiki.'

'She's well.'

'Mpanjo.'

'He's well.'

'Maka.'

'He's well.'

'Ngea of lies.'

'She's well. She said I should greet you.'

He touched her belly.

'Is he still there?'

She laughed. 'Yes,' she said.

And he took her hand, went with her into the hut, locked the door and then she followed him willingly to the room.

But her return meant more conflicts for all of them.

He told her of Ewudu that very night.

'What?' she asked, outraged. 'Ewudu? In this bed?'

'Yes,' he said with unusual humility.

Her first reaction was a desire to get up and go and sit in the parlour for the rest of the night and in the morning leave him never to return again. But she knew she couldn't go back to Bomono. At least not now. They would laugh at her; for she had

had to run away very early in the morning so as not to be seen. Only her aunt Ngea knew of her plan. She had approved of it 'since it looks as though he isn't going to come. What else can you do? Go to him. I know he won't shut his door against you. You have his child in your womb. Go and don't mind what they say.'

All the others were against Ngoso; and since the day she arrived back home three weeks ago, with a swollen mouth, they had said all sorts of wicked things against him.

At first Njale used to join them whenever they were abusing him; but after the first week she began to think of him again, and whenever they abused him she remained silent, an attitude which made most of them furious, especially the young men of the family. They couldn't understand why she had suddenly changed and was apparently for him again.

When finally she couldn't bear it any more and Ngoso still hadn't come to beg her parents so that she might return with him, she went and talked to her aunt. That was when they decided on the lie she was to tell should she see him in Mudeka Market. They hadn't been very sure that it would work; but since they could find no other means of making him come to Bomono, they said they would try the lie.

It didn't work and so she had had to throw her pride to the winds and run the risk of turning the whole family, with the exception of her actress of an aunt, against her. And here she was only to learn that Ewudu had been sleeping in that very bed in which she was now sleeping with him and that she had gone away for a few days and would be returning.

'When did you say she would be coming back?' she asked with surprising calm.

'Next week,' he said.

She didn't say anything. She would wait for her. That was all she could do — just wait for that 'little thing,' she thought. 'I'll

teach her.' And then she heard herself saying aloud, quite involuntarily, 'she will see.'

'What will she see?'

'Nothing,' she said and turned her back to him.

19

She sulked throughout that night, throughout the following
day and the next and the next.

Ngoso knew she wanted him to choose between his child and
Ewudu who was probably barren; for, after all, hadn't Makole
said the other day that Ewudu had spoken wistfully in the beach
in Mongo about the fact that all women were having children
with the exception of herself? And he knew from experience that
once a woman began to talk like that it meant she had reason
to believe that she might never be a mother. And yet Ngoso
felt he loved Ewudu just as much as he loved the child in Njale's
womb.

No, he couldn't choose. He would wait and see. He knew
violence was ahead. But he didn't look at it in terms of blood.
When he looked at the future in connection with the two women,
he could see only tears which one of them would certainly have
to shed, if not both of them.

He could see Njale beating Ewudu who was much younger
than Njale; and he saw himself intervening on Ewudu's side

and Njale's hardness giving way. He saw her turning away, crying, feeling alone, feeling betrayed.

'Njale,' he said. 'You know a man can marry two women. My father had two.'

'Is it again about Ewudu that you are bursting my ears?'

'Yes,' he said. 'I'll marry you, Njale. And later, we shall make plans about Ewudu. There are never enough people in any family.'

Something happened in his heart when once more he reflected on the possibility of Ewudu being barren. But what can that do? he thought. Even if she gives me no children I shall always love her. I'll marry her; and then, she's still too young for me to worry about her womb. Why won't she have children?

'Njale,' he said, 'learn to accept Ewudu.'

'Haven't I told you that we shall see?' she asked, her look bitter. 'Let her come. If she doesn't find her way back to wherever she came from don't call me a woman. Have you forgotten that Ndongo too was here?'

'You have reminded me of something,' he said. 'I have to take her potatoes to her. That's what I'll do tomorrow. Shall we go down together?'

'Who?' she asked, wild. 'That I Njal' Epukepuk' a Mbanja Mikondo shall leave this house that I'm going to take potatoes to your lover — '

'But they are her potatoes.'

'A-Ngoso, you are not well.'

'It's you who are not well,' he said, almost losing his temper. 'You think when people say you aren't hospitable, they are praising you?'

'But what can that do to me?'

'I've always told you that you must like people. Hate is not profitable. Tomorrow I'll go to Bojongo; and from there to Duala. I shall return with Ewudu and you must welcome her with an open heart.'

'And if I don't?'

'We shall see.'

'But that's what I said. We shall see.'

That evening Makole returned from Duala. When Njale heard his voice she went to the room, not wanting to see him. She had even refused to go and see his child.

'*A*-ugly-faced Njale!' Makole called.

'Who told you that she had come back?'

'People who came to the market from Bomono,' Ngoso's friend said. 'So all our sadness was for nothing. *Uweh!* What great liars Pongo people are!'

'That's nothing to talk about.'

'Has she been to see her man?' — that is, Inon's child, since he bore Ngoso's name. 'No?'

'No.'

'Why?'

'Ask her.'

'When did she come back?'

'Five days ago.'

'Is she still so foolish?'

'But she was born foolish,' Ngoso said.

'Born foolish,' Njale growled in the room.

'Listen to her,' Makole sneered.

As the two friends were leaving the hut, Makole said:

'*A*-Ngoso.'

'Yes?'

'They say Ewudu's man has promised to hack you to pieces.'

Ngoso burst out laughing. 'Is that so?' he asked.

'Don't joke,' his friend said. 'He's bought a new machete. He's been sharpening it for days. They say he shows it to everyone that it is with that machete that he's going to tap your blood.'

'But let him come,' Ngoso said. 'A Bakweriman, did they

125

tell him that we live on a mountain? That we own horses and cows and pigs? Doesn't he know that we are water people and we move about in canoes?'

'I think it would be necessary that you be a bit careful.'

'Let him come,' Ngoso said. 'I'll hold his head in the water. He'll drink his own couple of gulps. I've always said that. Let him come. He's going to tap my blood, his impudence!'

'Don't think it's a joke. Etaka says if you have any sense in your head you shouldn't bring Ewudu back. They say her man is too violent.'

'Wonderful,' Ngoso said. 'I'll bring Ewudu back. Why won't I bring her back? I'm going down tomorrow.'

He was in Bojongo the following evening.

'*Uweh!*' Ndongo said when, sitting with another girl on the verandah, she saw Ngoso. 'O-o-o-ho, Aunty Longele, what a sudden visitor!'

'Who?' Ngoso's middle-aged step-aunt asked, coming out of her house which was on the other side of the road from the beach. She saw Ngoso. 'My husband!'

They had been twelve in their family, all children of the same parents. Ngoso's father had married the eldest girl who died eleven years later. She was buried in the cemetary in Bojongo which had once been a town but which was now a small village.

Of the twelve Longele was the youngest and Ngoso had been in love with her since he was a boy and she a young girl. She was the woman he would have loved to marry; but this was impossible because she was the sister of a woman who had been his father's wife.

Some of Ngoso's early quarrels with his brother Mbongo had been about Longele. Ngoso was always very jealous whenever she was particularly nice to Mbongo; this made him very angry. He imagined she was loving his brother instead of him. And the fact that for some reason she had never been married and wasn't likely to be married now that she was no longer so young only strengthened Ngoso's feelings for her. Somewhere in his mind he was her husband and the fact that she called him 'my husband,' with a kind of sincere tenderness gave him so much pleasure that over the years he had secretly wished she would never be married. He didn't even want her to have a lover; and Longele la Bamendepo was such a beautiful woman!

20

Ndongo said she would accompany him to Duala. She had a few things she wanted to buy. And she'd take some of the potatoes to the market. She had given three baskets of potatoes to his step-aunt.

'So you'll have to load the canoe all over again,' he said. 'You should have thought of that earlier.'

'I know,' Ndongo said. 'But it doesn't matter. We still have time. I'll begin taking them down to the beach at once.'

'But I must warn you,' he told her, 'that tomorrow we shall be returning with Ewudu.'

'Is she coming to meet you in the market?'

'Yes.'

'But what can that do?'

'You are a very good girl,' he said. 'You are never jealous.'

'*Eyaye!*' she laughed. 'Because I don't show it?'

They set out from Bojongo very late that evening with almost half of the canoe-load of potatoes he had brought from the farm. He planned to reach Mambanda around midnight, wait for the first cocks and then begin to cross the sea on the other side of which Duala stands, a prosperous, modern, gay and intense city.

He paddled and paddled. But he didn't paddle as he would have been paddling had he been alone in the canoe. He paddled only when he wasn't talking to Ndongo.

They met many canoes waiting for the dawn at Mambanda; they were waiting for the most favourable time to cross the sea.

Ngoso paddled his canoe between two canoes which were waiting for the dawn and the tide.

Some of the canoes were loaded with plantains; others with firewood for the market in Duala. They were all waiting for the tide and the time when the sea would be less windy.

Ngoso waited with the other canoemen.

Then it began to rain. It rained heavily. Ndongo had expected it would rain at Mambanda. It always rained there. So she had brought an umbrella with her. She opened it and held it over her head and asked Ngoso to come and sit with her. But he wouldn't leave his place at the helm. He said he wasn't salt that dissolved in the rain.

'Only make sure our bags are well covered.'

She leaned forward and touched the leaves he had carefully put over the potatoes and the bags.

'They won't get wet,' she assured him.

The rain was rough. It came down with fast, biting winds; and holding the umbrella in one hand she bailed out the rain-water with the other hand. It was still raining when the cocks began to crow and Ngoso and the other canoemen began to pull their canoes out of Mambanda.

He had the impression the rain had entered right into his bones. He hoped the day would be a bit sunny.

Although it was still raining, the winds were less strong now and everybody thought the crossing would be easy.

The canoes had left Mambanda in a group; but by the time they had come out of the creek they had separated and this was the sea and the wind was blowing at a terrific speed, coming from the ocean on their right. In front of them, on the other side of the sea, the lights of Duala glittered like stars in a storm and Ngoso wondered about Ewudu. Was she asleep, enjoying the sound of the rain on the roof?

Or was she out, dancing with that friend of hers who sold her body for money?

He paddled, not wanting to think of Ewudu and the men on the other side of the sea.

Ships were in the harbour. More were sailing in from the ocean. They could see their lights.

And then the waves began to lift his canoe very high and he paddled and paddled and it was as if he hadn't been shivering from the rain and the cold winds.

Saline luminosity stirred by his paddling!

Ndongo folded the umbrella so that she might not lose it to the winds. It was impossible to keep an open umbrella in one's hands when the atmosphere was so stormy, the sea so rough. But he beat the waves.

After an hour or so of careful, though energetic paddling through the disturbed sea, here they were, between two ships berthed along the wharf.

And it had ceased to rain.

He paddled into the canal that led to the market. They passed under a bridge. Then another bridge.

It was still dark. But Duala doesn't sleep. Cars. From time to time one shot past, leaving its sound behind.

The air smelt of foreign foods and of decaying onions and of petrol and of other things characteristic of commercial ports. And there was the smell of coal from the railway station on the other side of the market.

He found a place where he shoved his canoe and putting down his paddle he realised that he had caught a cold. His head was aching again.

She removed her dress and her silk headscarf from her bag. She was shivering. She put back the dress and the headscarf in the bag and took his bag and turned towards the helm.

'Take,' she said, 'your bag. Take off those wet things at once.'

'Thank you,' he said, reaching for the bag.

Many men and women were on the waterfront; and every now and then one heard the voice of a little boy or girl. Most of the people were either fishermen or, like Ngoso, farmers. This was where, as in Mudeka, they made money, not much; but it was money all the same.

Ngoso undressed. He folded the wet clothes he had been wearing and put them in a basket. He put on a clean pair of shorts and a fine shirt. In Duala one had to be properly dressed when haggling with those women who arrived in the market in the morning. They were sophisticated women who made faces at everything as if the whole world was nasty with the exception of themselves. One had to be properly dressed in order to feel smart and talk gaily, proudly, with them. Some of them arrived in cars. And some even had paid servants who carried their shopping bags for them.

The dawn had begun to circumscribe the street lights. He tied his loin-cloth round his waist.

Meanwhile Ndongo was also changing into a another dress.

The street lights were shining less and less brightly. A chalky dawn from the point of view of colour and not the substance of the unfolding day.

Ndongo tied her headscarf, and Ngoso asked her to pass him her wooden comb and the bottle of *mananga* oil.

'I don't know why I forgot my comb,' he said, not liking the fact that he would have to comb his hair with a woman's comb. But it doesn't matter, he said to himself.

She gave him the comb and the bottle of oil and he raised his loin-cloth and put the black palm kernel oil on his feet and legs and rubbed them vigorously, right up to his thighs. He rubbed one foot, leg and thigh; and then the other foot, leg and thigh. The oil made them feel a bit warm.

Then he lowered his loin-cloth and taking a little *mananga* in his left palm, he rubbed it against the palm of his right hand. He rubbed both hands briskly and then he rubbed them on his overgrown hair after which, and without having put more oil in his palm he rubbed his arms, one, with the palm of his right hand, and then the other arm with the left palm. In spite of the headache and the fever he wanted to look smart when they would be selling the potatoes.

By nine o'clock the market was full. It was noisier than Mudeka market for there were cars and lorries here, honking and groaning, their exhaust pipes leaving smoke behind as they tried to move through the crowd.

People talked and talked. With the exception perhaps of one or two albinos everybody in the market in Mudeka was black; but here there were white people, especially white women. Some had red-pimpled faces, because of the mosquitoes. Sometimes you pitied them. They didn't look very happy. But there were others who had smooth faces, and who looked very well-kept and happy too. Some came to the market alone, carrying straw bags in which they put the things they bought. Others however, came with their stewards.

The rich black women looked more sophisticated than the white women. And the Africans were at their ease, gorgeously dressed, enjoying the fact that they were spending money and they looked ostentatious and very proud whereas the white women seemed to be spending their money grudgingly and they looked self-conscious. They were nervous. They took short, quick steps as soon as they found the way before them a bit clear. Most of them wore tight-fitting skirts which made them take very short steps. Sometimes though, you saw one who walked with ease, almost like an African woman.

And Ngoso and Ndongo sold the potatoes.

The sun touched the roofs of the market stalls. Apart from a few shops owned by Europeans who ran them with the help of their black assistants, most of the shops were owned by Africans and there were rows of makeshift stalls which were like kiosks.

Some women traders spread their wares on the pavements. They sold among other things vegetables, oil, fruits, and things like pepper and other spices.

The noise. The cars. Ngoso was glad because people were buying their potatoes. And as he had been thinking of Ewudu while he was selling plantains in Mudeka so he was thinking of her now, already seeing her in the shop where they had decided she would wait for him around noon today.

From the wharf a ship sounded a cynical siren announcing her impending departure for Europe or maybe for another part of the world; but to most of the people in the market that day every ship arriving in Duala was from Europe and every ship leaving the port was returning to the West.

By noon they had finished selling the potatoes and the siren of the saw-mill on the other side of the market sounded. It was noon! And to Ngoso that meant Ewudu.

'That's noon,' he said to Ndongo.

'So you are going to meet Ewudu?' she asked.

'Yes,' he said. 'I shall bring her and we shall go to the market together, the three of us — Ngos'a Mbedi and his two women!'

She smiled and he too smiled but with an effort because he was feverish and his head was aching more and more.

'How?' an assistant asked him at the shop. 'You came to look for Ewudu?'

'Yes.'

'She's gone to N'kongsamba.'

'What?'

'She's gone to N'kongsamba,' the shop assistant said.

He was in a white shirt and a white pair of shorts.

A man and a woman walked up to the shop assistant who was selling cloth and valises outside. The woman felt one print with her fingers, then another and then another.

'Gone to N'kongsamba,' Ngoso said to himself, not wanting to believe what he had just been told.

The woman's fingers returned to the first print she had felt.

'Yes,' the young man in a white shirt and white pair of shorts said, his eyes on the customer. 'She came here yesterday and said we should tell you that she's gone to N'kongsamba.' And then to the woman: 'They are all very good. I have the best prints in the market.' The woman raised her face to look at him, her fingers still on one of the prints. 'It's the truth. You can go and look if you wish.'

'Is that so?'

'I am telling you. Go; but I know you will come back. Our prints are wonderful.'

'I don't understand,' Ngoso sighed.

'What do you not understand?' asked the shop assistant.

'What?' an older person asked from the shop. 'Is it Ewudu?'

'Yes,' the assistant said. 'Look at this one,' he said to the woman.

'She's gone to N'kong,' the man inside the shop said, leaning on the counter. 'She was here yesterday with her friend, a

Bamoun girl. It's with her that she went. She said she couldn't miss the opportunity. They went by car. It looks as though that is the first time she's visiting N'kong.'

'Come,' the shop assistant said to the woman, holding her arm.

'But I thought you said I should go and look elsewhere,' the woman said while her man was smiling. 'You said I should go and look at what other shops have and that I shall come back.'

'It's true, *a-nyango*,' the young man coaxed. 'Go anywhere in the whole of this market, you'll come back because our prints are the best.'

All over the market traders said the same thing; their wares were the best.

'Then let me go.'

'Look at this one. Look at this one. It would suit you. Touch it again. You see?'

The woman laughed. 'You people,' she said and looked at her man; or maybe he was her brother.

'So, I have gone,' Ngoso said, turning to go.

'She said I should tell you that she heard that your woman had come back; so what was she coming to do over there? She said she didn't like quarrels. So she was going to N'kongsamba. She's gone.' He wasn't looking at Ngoso. 'They left yesterday afternoon.'

'But what happened?' the man inside the shop asked.

'What again?'

'Ewudu said you had been told that your woman was dead.'

Ngoso laughed in spite of himself.

'That was what we heard,' he said just as the proprietor of the shop rode in on a bicycle.

He shook Ngoso's hand and asked him about his farm.

'The farm is going on fine,' Ngoso said.

And then the proprietor asked him if there wasn't any message for him.

'None,' Ngoso said. 'And you over here, the wife and the children?'

'By the grace of God we all are well,' he said and went into the shop.

'You like it?' the woman's husband asked; or maybe he wasn't her husband.

The shop assistant already had a pair of scissors in his fingers. The woman made faces and shrugged her shoulders.

'It isn't bad,' she said.

'Then take it,' the man said.

She asked for the price. The shop assistant told her. She looked at her man again. He nodded in a boastful manner.

'How many metres?' asked the young man in a white pair of shorts and white shirt, about to cut the cloth.

Ngoso walked down the row of shops, feeling angry and ill.

In those shops one could buy everything from dressing material, valises, basins, lanterns, fishing hooks and twine to stock fish, rice and buckets and matchetes and axes. There were lots and lots of other wares.

He and Ndongo were among the many peasants who felt like strangers in Duala even though some of them had relatives, even their own children, working there, or going to school. To them it was the most dazzling city in the world, that is, whenever they didn't think of those cities of the west to which the ships sailing from Duala went.

Feeling very disturbed and feeling ill, Ngoso crossed a street. He was returning to the canalside where he had left Ndongo.

It was so noisy here; no peace of mind, no surprise voice rising to sing of women and of hope like those he used to hear on his farm; like his own voice, for he too used to sing of women and of hope while paddling on the river.

'Sing, man of joy, sing,' women bathing in the river used to sing in reply to his voice and they beat the water with their tender hands, making the river sound like drums.

That was to the north with the sun shining overhead and whether or not there were clouds.

But here he was in a different world, a world without egrets, a world without forest echoes, without floods, without farms. To town folks the market was their farm and money their hoes and matchetes. And because he was sad it felt even a more different world to him. To think that he had taken her from that man only to come and lose her in Duala! How could he be sure she wouldn't misbehave in N'kongsamba?

He wondered whether or not he should go to her sister's place in Bonebela. No, he thought, there was no point. And when he thought of the woman he had left on the farm and how strained their relations had been before he left because of this same Ewudu who maybe was dancing and drinking beer that very moment with other men, he felt very miserable in his heart.

'But where is Ewudu?' Ndongo asked him when he got to the canoe.

'She's gone to N'kongsamba,' he told her.

She gave a little derisive laugh; then noticing the pain which showed on his face, she frowned, alarmed.

'Aren't you feeling well?'

'I'm a bit feverish,' he said. 'I think it's last night's rain.'

'And will you be able to cross today?'

'Why not? Unless you want to stay in Duala.'

'No,' she said. 'It's because of you. You look really ill.'

'It's nothing,' he said. 'Go and buy whatever you want to buy. We must cross in a few moments. I don't know why I am feeling like this. Go to the market. Hurry up.'

She took a bag and rose from the canoe. She smoothed the seat of her dress with the back of her right hand.

136

'I'm coming,' she said.

'Wait,' he called after her. 'Take some money,' he said, putting his hand into the hip pocket of his pair of shorts. 'Buy aunty some rice and salt fish. I also need some for myself.' That was because of Njale. If he should return from Duala without rice and salt fish she would be very angry with him. 'And buy some bread and sugar.'

'Leave,' she said. 'I have some money.'

'It doesn't matter,' he said. 'It's not every day that you will sell potatoes. Take — '

'I say leave,' she said and went off.

Ngoso sat in the canoe for a while and then he thought of cigarettes. He got up and went into the market where he bought three packets and two boxes of matches. He didn't want to buy more because of the customs people.

2 I

Whenever Njale thought that Ngoso would be arriving on the farm that evening with Ewudu she felt so angry and helpless that she feared she was going out of her mind. Why was he doing that to her? He who was himself so jealous, why couldn't he understand that jealousy was a kind of death? Why was he driving her to a premature death? What had she done against him? Why didn't he love her anymore. What had Ewudu that she, Njale, hadn't?

But if jealousy could drive one to one's death, it was not itself a kind of death in spite of what Njale imagined. But it was true that it could be suicidal through restlessness. That was the state in which she now was.

And they would be arriving that evening!

No; she simply couldn't bear to wait for them. She would have to go away. She just had to leave the farm. She would go to Missaka and stay with Dikodu and his wife. When they arrive and they don't find me in the house, she said to herself, I'll see what they will do. If he doesn't come to beg me at Dikodu's I shan't come back here. Never!

She locked the back door and then the front door and put the key between two thatches on the verandah and went out. She walked under the cocoa trees, passed the little burial ground and left his farm behind.

The flood had already subsided, leaving the riverbanks covered with silt. The reeds and all the grasses of the riverbanks wore mud and riverbirds paced the banks, looking at the water as if surprised that it was more or less clear again.

It was just after noon and in the east the sun was making a determined effort to keep on shining. But it didn't look as though it was succeeding.

The river was on her right. She wished she could hold her long face over it. She wished the river was a mirror. She wanted to see how swollen her eyes had become for she had wept throughout the night.

But now that the first floods were over, the surface of the river was once more far away down the headland along which she was walking. And the water wasn't a mirror anyway. Yes, she was going out of her mind. Yes, people would talk about it; that she Njal' Epukepuke went mad because of a Mongoman. That was what he was doing to her just because he wanted all the women in the world, his pride!

She walked and walked. But what has that Ewudu that I haven't, she wondered when she got to the beach opposite Missaka. She saw herself as she was: the long face, the stout, shapely body, the large breasts, her long thighs which she used to wrap round him! She had to be generous towards herself. It is not true that I am not pretty, she said aloud, trying to convince herself. 'It's not true at all. Then why is he doing this to me?'

And then almost involuntarily she saw Ewudu in her mind. She was a ripe woman all right; but being so small, so sure of herself, she looked almost innocent, like a bold virgin. She hasn't even breasts, Njale thought, almost triumphantly. She hasn't even buttocks. Then what does he see in her? What attracts him to her so much?

She raised her face in the air and called:

'O-o-ho!'

She waited, listening to the echo of her own voice. When it dissolved in the wind, she called again:

'O-o-ho!'

'O!' someone answered from the village.

'Come-o!'

A few moments later she saw Mbedi on the opposite beach. The boy was fourteen. He held a paddle in one hand and went to one of the canoes which were in the beach. He unchained it and putting the chain in the canoe its links made a trickling sound as if gravels were being poured into the canoe.

Then Njale heard Ngombe calling:

'A-Mbedi! Mbedi, wait for me.'

But Mbedi didn't wait.

'Sita Njale,' he said, 'is it you?'

'Yes,' Njale said.

Mbedi was soon paddling upstream until it seemed as though he was going to somewhere else and not to the beach which was exactly opposite the one from which he had taken the canoe.

But that was because he wanted to avoid the swift current in the heart of the river; by paddling upstream and then swinging the canoe southwards as he was now doing, aiming the prow at the beach on which Njale was waiting, the current would help him into the beach.

Njale saw Ngombe who was much younger than Mbedi. He erupted on the beach, a little paddle in one hand, the other supporting his loin-cloth which was loosely tied about his waist. It was lower on one hip than on the other. He burst out crying when he saw that Mbedi had left without him.

The boy wept, his little paddle in one hand and then supporting his loin-cloth with the other hand.

As soon as Mbedi had ferried her across, Njale hurried to Dikodu's place, hoping to find comfort there. And as soon as they began to converse, Ewudu was on her lips.

'He brought her right to my bed,' she complained, seeking their sympathy. 'And this evening he's bringing her back.'

'Did he go to Duala?'

'Yes,' Njale said. 'He went to bring his wife.'

'It's your fault,' Old Dikodu said.

'How is it her fault?' his wife asked.

'If they hadn't told that lie he wouldn't have brought her from Mudeka.'

'Go away,' Mwenen said.

The old man laughed slyly without looking at his wife.

'He thought you wouldn't be seen on the farm again,' he said to Njale. 'And will you blame him? It's only in stories that the dead return from the grave. And you didn't meet each other in a story. You knew each other in life.'

'Then why didn't he come when he heard that I was dead?'

'But you weren't dead,' said Old Dikodu, looking at her, a frown on his face as if he was going to get angry. 'It was a lie.'

'But at the time did he know that it was a lie?'

'Something in him must have known,' Dikodu said. 'If one's body is heavy about a trip one has to make it means something is not altogether straight ahead. I am sure his body told him that you weren't dead; otherwise he would have gone to Bomono the same day he heard about it in Mudeka.'

'If he knew I was still alive,' Njale argued, having found what she thought was a weak point in the old man's case on behalf of his late friend's son, 'why then did he bring her? I thought you said he brought her because the dead never return?'

She looked at the story-teller's wife for support; but Mwenen didn't say anything.

'When someone's body tells him something, he can never be very sure about it,' said the old man who wasn't treating Njale seriously; in fact he was amused by her worries because he thought that she wasn't herself without some blame in the matter. 'And then,' he pursued, 'even if he knew you weren't dead, how was he to know that you would be returning? When you went away did you leave behind a promise of the day you would be returning?'

'Now is it right that you should be defending him as if what he is doing is right?' Mwenen asked her husband to Njale's great relief.

She had begun to get impatient with them and was blaming herself for having come at all. She had even begun to hate the couple. Now, however, with Mwenen apparently siding with her, she began to feel better. It was no longer a question of Mongo people defending a Mongoman against a Pongo woman. It was a question of a man defending another man against the just complaints of a woman and another woman siding with the persecuted woman.

'I am only saying what is,' old Dikodu said. 'And,' he said to his wife, 'you heard what he told us the other day.'

'What did he tell you?' Njale asked, saying to herself: look at his shiny head!

Mwenen who had been going about the house, doing one thing or the other, drew up a stool and sat down in front of Njale.

'It looks as though you have been turning your back to him,' she said, searching Njale's eyes, wishing she would contradict her because they all knew that sometimes Ngoso lied.

'What did you want me to do?' Njale asked, 'when, as soon as I arrived, he began to talk to me of that useless thing.'

That wasn't entirely true. They had spent an intense afternoon together. He had loved her and shown her that he still loved her. They had never enjoyed each other as much as they did that afternoon and then it was while he was eating the evening meal she had prepared for him that she had noticed that he was worried.

'What's the matter?' she had asked him, becoming very worried herself.

'Nothing,' he had replied.

'Tell me,' she had insisted and for the first time she had appeared to be after all a tender and sensible woman. 'There's something on your mind.'

'Nothing.'

'*A*-Ngoso,' she had said, putting down the piece of fish she was about to eat. 'Don't annoy me.'

There had been a note of despair in her voice which had disarmed his reticence.

'I'll tell you later,' he said and drank some water.

And then all of a sudden she didn't want to hear him talk about it, whatever it was. He ceased worrying while she continued to worry until even before they went to bed he had to ask:

'What's the matter?'

'Nothing,' she had replied in her turn.

He knew it was because she was afraid to hear him talk, later, as he had promised her, of another woman; for what else could he have had on his mind after such a great afternoon with her? He was sure Njale knew it was about another woman that he was thinking.

He had almost decided against discussing Ewudu but because he had fallen in love with Njale all over again he couldn't hold back anything from her; he had to talk about the other woman. By talking about her he would feel free; he would feel himself again — master of his women. And so when they went to bed he talked to her of Ewudu and that spoilt their night and the other nights which followed before he left yesterday for Bojongo and Duala.

Mwenen shrugged her shoulders; she looked very sorry for Njale. She could see she was regretting having turned her back on Ngoso.

Pity and regret sometimes go hand in hand. Mwenen had the strange feeling that Ngoso would never care for Njale again.

'Well,' said Dikodu, 'now he has gone to bring a woman who wouldn't turn her back on him.'

Ewudu's girlish body came to Njale's mind; and her face clouded. She looked at the old man, almost wishing he would say something which would lighten the burden left on her heart by what he had just said.

But Dikodu had spoken. He didn't intend to add another word to what he had just said. He rose and went to the backyard.

'Your father is right,' Mwenen said, meaning her husband was right. 'You shouldn't have done that. You know you have his child in your belly. And a man always wants to feel near his child. But if you turn your back on him how is he going to warm up his child? And a child likes to see its father touching its mother, you know. So if you do what you did you annoy the father and annoy the child as well.'

'But let him get annoyed.'

143

'Don't say that again,' Mwenen said. 'If you turn your back on him it's as if you are tearing him and his child apart. I don't know why you are killing yourself. You know you are going to be the mother of his child; and that would be the first child he'll be having since he began to run after women — '

'Who told you that?'

'He did,' the woman said. 'That was where he was sitting.'

'His first child?'

'Yes. And a man never forgets the mother of his child.'

'To a man like Ngoso who likes women so much what is a child to him?'

'Don't say that again. You don't know what that child means to him. You don't know what *you* mean to Ngoso because of that great thing you are going to do for him?'

'He doesn't seem to think it's a great thing,' Njale said as if disgusted, 'otherwise he wouldn't have beaten me the way he did. Ngoso? You don't know him.'

2 2

He suddenly forgot that he was ill. The thought that Njale was at home made him feel good. Because of her he was aware of the many other people he had in the world, and he felt even younger than he was. What a fine thing that he was going to be a father! He accidently bit his tongue. It hurt. They are calling

my name, he thought. Maybe it was Ewudu. It couldn't be Njale.
He saw her sitting on the verandah, morose, vindictive, staring
in front of her. And then he saw the young sao tree which, as
you were coming out of his hut, was on the right of his compound. It hadn't begun bearing fruit; but he was sure it would
next year or in two or three years' time. He had planted it
while he was a little boy. And then he saw the huge cactus on
the edge of his compound. It had been planted by his father.
He, Ngoso, had been only a child at the time; or maybe he
hadn't even been born. But he was sure it was his father who
had planted it. He couldn't remember his late parents ever having
discussed it with him. All he knew was that it had protective
powers and it was very old. He saw the sun of the dry season
and saw the shade under the sao tree. That would be in just
over six months' time. He would buy a pair of shoes for Njale.
He would make Ndongo wear it, because of the customs people.
He saw her sitting in the canoe with her feet in the new pair
of shoes. But she would have to be careful so they didn't get
wet. Njale would be happy about the shoes; and if it hadn't
been for the customs people he would have bought many other
things for her.

Then he thought of Inon's child. He would buy a little shirt
and two pairs of socks for his namesake. He felt very happy,
seeing the sun of the next dry season. A bright sun in a sky
of very white clouds. And in the afternoon winds clumps of
wild cotton from the buma trees!

All that in his imagination. And he saw Njale not as his
lover but as his wife sitting under the shade of the sao tree.
I must buy a bottle of strong drink for the knocking of her
father's door. Yes, he had to initiate negotiations for the marriage. She would be the only woman he would marry.

He stopped before a stall and bought a shirt for Makole's
son; and then the socks. He wondered whether or not he

should wait until two o'clock when the big shops would re-open. No, he thought, and went to another stall where he bought a cheap pair of shoes because he couldn't afford to buy one which was more expensive. He hadn't enough money and there was that bottle of strong drink for Njale's father. He saw himself as the father of many children and Njale as their mother. He saw the farm full of people — noisy, gay; children running all over the place, shouting and playing and once more he saw the sun.

He was living his vision of tomorrow and the months and years after tomorrow. And he saw himself growing old, contented and very wise and now he was sorry to have gone to the camp to steal Ewudu from her man. He would never do such a thing again. Never! And, coming to think of it, he reflected, it was after all a good thing that she had gone away. 'Take off my wife's shoes,' he said after they had passed the customs officers who had stopped them in the canal.

Ndongo a Mesanedimabu turned and looked at him over her shoulder, an expression of hurt humility in her eyes. She smiled weakly and then when she noticed the frown on his face she began to worry. She took off the shoes and wrapping them in a piece of paper she put them in his travelling bag.

'Are you feeling very ill?' she asked him.

'No,' he said.

He was determined to sleep on his farm that night. It was a pity that he was feverish and it was as if something was splitting his head from inside. It would have been wonderful, if he hadn't been ill, to arrive on the farm and talk to Njale about their future. It would have been a great night of reconciliation in love. He wouldn't waste the least time in Bojongo. They had been lucky, he reflected. That headache! They had been lucky because the customs people had been very perfunctory in their search of the canoe.

146

'I don't know why I didn't bring a paddle,' Ndongo said.
'Why?'

'I would have helped you.'

'Look at her eyes,' he said, still wearing the frown.

She didn't smile as she would have done had he not been ill. She knew that being a man he was only trying to pretend that the fever was nothing. But she knew he was suffering.

And now they were on the sea, the sea which had been so rough during the night. They could hear the receding drone of the cranes that hauled goods out of the ships while other cranes loaded the same ships and other ships with some of the land's products; cocoa, cotton from the north, logs, bananas – in Bonaberi – coffee and a few other agricultural products.

The receding drone of the cranes and of the cars and lorries and the whining sound of the saw-mill.

And then the sodden sun suddenly crawled out of the clouds in which the winds had wrapped it for the last hour or so. It held such light and heat as it still could hold – given the season – over the sea. The sky was high and blue where it was bare, and low where it was cloudy.

Ngoso began to feel Bojongo was too far away. But luckily for him the sea was calm.

The sky had clouded even the more when they reached Bojongo. They met a woman on the beach. She was washing dishes, plates and two or three spoons and a fork or two. She asked them what news they had of Duala.

'No bad news,' Ngoso said, alighting. 'And here?'

'Nothing bad,' said the woman.

Mudskippers ran about under the mangrove trees. They crawled nervously in and out of the water. A sprinkling of sea-shells was on the sandy beach on the right and left of which was soft, black mud – the play-ground of the mudskippers. And there were crabs. And the whole place smelt of fish slime

147

and of mud and of the salty scent of the breath of the ocean.

Urged on by the winds the mangrove trees shook their branches at the cloudy sky as if they didn't want the rain which seemed about to fall.

The way Ngoso was feeling he simply couldn't paddle to his farm that afternoon. It was impossible and he felt very frustrated because he had imagined himself arriving and taking Njale by the hand and making her sit down. Then he put his hand into his bag and brought out the pair of shoes and gave them to her and then he showed her the bottle and said it was for her father; and then the announcement that he would go to her people the following week.

'And Ewudu?' he had heard Njale ask in his imagination.

He had decided that he wouldn't tell her what had happened. He would wait until he had returned from her father's place; then he would tell her about N'kongsamba and the message Ewudu had left for him at the shop.

In spite of the blankets Ndongo heaped on him when they got to her place Ngoso still said he was feeling cold, and he was shivering.

Ndongo was alarmed. She was afraid. She wanted to be with him. She didn't want to leave him; but there was his step-aunt who must know at once that he was ill. She would prepare some medicine for him.

Ndongo wanted to go and call her; but she didn't want to leave him alone in the house. She sat down on the edge of the bed, tears running down her cheeks.

She began to sob. The fever was sinking into his sides, cooking them. He opened his eyes and saw that Ndongo was crying. He didn't want her to be frightened. He didn't want to shift some of his suffering on her head. He must reassure her. He must say something consoling.

'Why are you crying?' he asked her. 'Don't cry. I won't

die. What have I done to die now? Don't cry.'

She got up, wiping her eyes.

'Where are you going?' he asked because her being there made him feel better. To be ill and to be alone was more than he could bear.

'I'm going to tell Aunty Longele,' she said.

'Yes, go and tell her,' he said.

After a while he felt someone put a tender hand on his shoulder.

'Ngoso, *a*-Ngoso.'

It was Longele.

'*E*,' he answered, '*e, e*.'

'What did you do to yourself?'

'I don't know, I don't know.'

'Besides the fever,' the woman asked, 'do you feel any pains?'

'In the head,' he moaned, 'in the head.'

'We are coming,' she said. 'Ndongo, let's go and find some herbs.'

Left alone Ngoso began to ask himself why should he die?

'Ndongo,' he called feebly.

The girl came in.

'Did you call me?'

'Yes,' he said. 'I forgot. We should have visited Makole's mother. You know she is ill and in hospital in Duala.'

'Why are you just thinking of it now?'

'I don't know,' he moaned. 'I don't know.'

'Ndongo, let's go,' his step-aunt said.

Why should he die? he wondered. He wanted to continue living because he wanted to have a lot of children and wanted to see them growing up. He wanted to live and he loved the Mungo River — its two seasons, especially the dry season, its birds, its days and its nights and dawns! He loved its women who came and went away and returned and came and went. He loved life.

149

It seemed to him that they were staying too long. What kind of herbs were they looking for?

Outside the day was dying a premature death, evening closing in already, pushed forward by irascible winds carrying heavy rainclouds.

Then he heard the voices of the two women.

Ndongo and his step aunt returned with a great quantity of herbs. The girl opened the door which led to the backyard and his aunt went to the kitchen. And Ndongo went to the room.

'How are you feeling?' she asked, sitting on the bed.

'Bad,' he confessed. 'Bad, very bad.'

· She sighed and rose from the bed and went to the kitchen where she met Longele making the fire. She had put the herbs in a big pot in which she had added some water.

A flame, followed by others rose from the firebrands — chubby flames and slimmer ones, yellow and supple. And the fire sparked.

Longele who smiled easily and was very kind lifted the pot and put it on the stone tripod of the fireside; then she straightened up, the back of her right hand on her hip.

'*Ate*,' she moaned, smiling. 'Old age.'

In the past Ndongo would have laughed at such good-natured self-mockery, especially as Longele wasn't really that old. But today, with Ngoso ill, she didn't even smile. It was as if she hadn't heard.

'You think he'll get better?' she asked, staring into the fire.

Longele saw the flames dancing in the girl's eyes.

She smiled.

'Is that why you are crying?' she asked. 'My husband will get well. It's a little fever. You'll see tomorrow. If they tell you that he had been ill you will say no. Today will be like a bad dream. Don't cry. He will continue to give you what he used to give you.'

She laughed and Ndongo turned away.

'You have started,' she mumbled.

'You and your shyness,' Longele said, 'what is there to be ashamed of? You are no longer a child. You are a woman.' And then she said she was coming. She was going to her place to mix some medicine for him. 'Make the fire,' she added and went out.

Later when she brought the pot of herbs in the room she asked Ndongo to bring a stool and a basin.

Longele put her hand on Ngoso's shoulder.

'Sit up,' she said coaxingly.

He liked the feel of her hand on his shoulder and he cursed death. Ndongo came in with a lantern. She left it on the floor and went out for the stool and basin.

Ngoso managed to sit up. The room, which had been smelling of the mustiness of weathering thatches and the humidity of the floor, was now full of the warm, vaporous smell of the herbs.

'My husband,' she whispered tenderly just before Ndongo came in with the stool and the basin.

Longele took the stool from the girl. She put it down by the pot of medicine. She also took the basin and leaned it against the wall.

Ndongo put the back of her hand on Ngoso's cheek.

'It's real fire that is in his body,' she said, shaking her head.

Longele approached the bed. 'No shame now,' she said and began to take off the blankets he was still wearing like a coat. Then she began to unbutton his shirt. But he shook himself in protest. He didn't want to be undressed. He would do it himself.

They watched him undress. Ndongo took his shirt from him.

'Bring me a towel,' he said.

When Ndongo gave him the towel, he passed it under his loin-cloth and tied it round his waist. Then he undid the loin-cloth and gave it to Ndongo. He moved to where the pot and stool were.

He sat down, his thighs apart with the big pot before him like a drum he was going to begin playing.

His step-aunt went behind him and holding him about the shoulders said he should move nearer to the pot. He held the stool with his left hand and moved forward unaided even though Longele's hands were about his shoulders.

'Ndongo, bring me the blankets,' she said, 'but first bring him something with which he will stir the herbs.'

The girl went out and came back with a short stick; but it was long enough to reach the bottom of the pot. She gave it to his aunt and then she passed the first blankets to her.

Longele covered Ngoso with the blanket. Then Ndongo held a second blanket to her. She covered it on him. And then a third. She added it on the other two.

Now she bent down and passed her right hand under the blankets. She touched the pot. She moved her fingers up its sooty sides to the lid which she drew towards her and then out of the blankets careful, however, not to let too much vapour escape. With the same care she introduced the stick into the pot and asked Ngoso to stir the herbs with it as soon as he felt the steam was cooling off.

She straightened up.

'That waist,' she moaned, her hand on her hip.

This time Ndongo smiled. Ngoso was being treated. There was hope.

23

News of Ngoso's illness reached his friend Makole four days later and he went to tell Njale.

'What do you want me to do?' she asked. 'Was it I who sent him to Bojongo?'

'*A-nyango*,' Makole heard a man's voice inside the hut, 'who is that?'

'It isn't Ngoso,' Njale said.

'Who is that?' Makole asked.

'Ewudu's man.'

'The Bakweriman?'

'Yes,' Njale said. 'So is Ewudu also in Bojongo?'

'I don't know,' Makole said. 'When did he come?'

'Two days ago.'

'What does he want?' Makole asked, lowering his voice.

'What does he want!' Njale said.

Ekema appeared in the doorway.

'Are you Ngoso's friend?' he asked.

'Yes,' Makole said.

'Where is he?'

'He says he's ill,' Njale said carelessly.

'And are you going to visit him?'

'Yes,' Makole said, wondering whether or not he shouldn't provoke him and beat him. Why was he so pompous? 'I'll go there this very afternoon. You want to come with me?' His voice was full of spite and he could feel Njale becoming nervous, fearing trouble. 'No?' Makole asked. 'You don't want to come with me? I thought you once sent a message that you were going to cut him to pieces. This is the time if you still have that machete of yours.'

'I still have it,' Ekema declared and went into the hut. He was soon out again with the machete. 'Go and tell him that I am waiting for him in his house. If he's going to be away for a month, I'll still be here; and if for a year I'll still be here. I am not alone. He left a woman in the house. She's taking very good care of me. Go and tell him that.'

Ekema glanced at Njale and Makole saw their eyes meet. He thought he saw them smile discreetly at each other as if at a secret and he was very sorry for this friend. How could one tell such a thing to a sick man?

'Njale,' he said, 'I am going down this afternoon.'

'With this rain?'

'I have to go and see him. If he isn't getting better I'll take him to the hospital in Duala. Get ready.'

'Get ready to do what?'

'You are coming down with me.'

'That Njal' Epukepuke shall leave this house that I am going to?' She felt too bitter even to finish what she was saying.

'I know you and Ndongo don't get on at all, but it is not because of that that you won't go and visit Ngoso. He is ill.'

'I'm not going.'

Makole was glad to find his friend not as ill as he had feared.

'If you had seen him two days ago!' Longele said.

'All my heart was full of fear,' Ndongo confessed. 'But God is not asleep.'

'Do you know if Mbongo knows?' Longele asked.

'I called in Mongo on my way here,' Makole said. 'I was told that he is away in the fishing port. But I sent a message to him.'

'Mbongo with fishing,' Longele said.

Ngoso hadn't failed to notice how excited Longele and Ndongo had become since Makole's arrival. They laughed more readily, especially his step-aunt.

Outside it wasn't raining any more and the sun even tried to shine; but it made a mess of the whole affair and had to give up its cloudy efforts.

'But why didn't Njale come?' Ndongo finally asked.

It had seemed to Makole as though that was a question they all had been avoiding since they saw him arrive without Njale. They had asked him about his wife and the child and he had told them that they were well, that Inon and his sister-in-law sent them greetings. 'Inon says you must get well quickly,' he had told Ngoso on arrival. But they hadn't said a word about Njale, the woman he had left in his hut six days ago. They must have been waiting for him to say something about her. But how could he? Especially in the presence of the two women?

Now all their eyes were on him. They were waiting to hear why that stout, heady woman hadn't come down to see the man who was the father of the child she was carrying in her belly. With her bad manners, why hadn't she come? He could see disappointment and wounded pride on Ngoso's face. The woman he had left at home hadn't come to see him after hearing of his illness.

Makole told them what Njale had said without mentioning Ekema, at least not while the women were there.

Ngoso's step-aunt clapped her hands, scandalised.

'What?' she cried, still clapping her hands. 'Or hasn't she a heart in her belly?'

Ndongo shook her head and went out of the room.

'Is that what she said?' Ngoso asked, smiling vaguely.

'Yes,' his friend replied.

'That thing,' Ngoso said, smiling, 'she will suffer in my hands.'

Without realising it he was preferring his present anger to the satisfaction he would have felt had she come to visit him. The anger provoked a return of his strength. He would beat her until her mouth was full of blood. He had never felt so cruel before. Njale? She would see, he swore in his thoughts. A woman he was going to marry wouldn't even come to see him on his sick-bed? No, she would see.

He was conscious of his strength and his masculine pride flowing back to him, fighting the weakness which would have been greater had she been there, behaving as though she feared he was going to die. And once more he saw tomorrow and the farm and his children of the future.

'Do you know Ekema?' Makole asked mysteriously when he was alone with Ngoso.

'Ekema?' Ngoso said, forming in his mind the image of his rival. A man in a suit. 'Ewudu's lover?'

'Yes,' Makole said. 'He's in your place.'

'Who?'

'I say Ekema. He's waiting for you.'

Ngoso sat up.

'Now I understand,' he sighed and then looking up, wild, he cried: 'Njale will feel my hands. Allowing him to sleep with her?'

'I don't think she'll do that kind of thing,' Makole said in spite of the insinuation which had been in Ekema's words. But he didn't want his friend to get too worked up. He wouldn't tell him what the man had said about Njale, he decided.

'Who told you she can't do such a thing?' Ngoso cried. 'Why didn't she come with you? If not because of him?' And then assailed by despair he cooled down. He was ill. 'Allowing him to sleep with her with my child in her,' he said, almost tear-fully because of the great advantage Ekema had over him. While he Ngoso was ill, Ekema was well.

'What's the matter?' his step-aunt asked, looking into the room. Ndongo was by her side.

Makole wouldn't talk.

'Someone is in my house,' Ngoso said.

'Who?'

'Ewudu's lover.'

'Is that why Njale didn't come?' Ndongo asked.

No one replied.

'Why is the world so trying?' his step-aunt asked.

They heard the pattering sound of hundreds of drops on the thatched roof; and then the wind was accompanying the rain.

'Makole,' Ngoso said.

'*E*?'

What do you say?'

'About what?'

Ngoso sighed, dropping his look and then raising it again to look at the women.

'Leave,' he said to his friend and leaned sideways and lay down and drew a blanket over him.

He was feeling very feverish again. Evening always did that to him. But today the fever was rougher. Could it be witchcraft?

'What did he say?' his step-aunt asked.

'Who?' Makole asked.

'That man.'

'He's waiting for Ngoso. He says even if Ngoso stays away for a year he would still be there with his machete.'

'With a machete?'

'He showed it to me.'

'He won't have to wait even for a day,' Ngoso said, sitting up again. 'I am going up this night.'

'*A*-,' his step-aunt said.

'Don't say that again,' Ndongo said, alarmed.

'Do you think you have recovered?' asked his step-aunt.

157

'You don't understand,' Ngoso said and he thought: Ekema, wetting my child's head!

'Who told you that we don't understand?'

'And look at the rain,' Ndongo said.

'Rain or no rain he won't leave this house,' Longele said.

Night fell and they all thought Ngoso had changed his mind. Food was prepared; but Ngoso wouldn't eat. They tried to persuade him. He wouldn't. He said he didn't feel like eating. In fact it wasn't only the illness and his thoughts of Ekema and Njale. It seemed to him that Makole had been eyeing Ndongo in a very suggestive way and somehow Ngoso had convinced himself that the girl liked his friend. The girl herself was very worried because she was among the few people who knew how jealous Ngoso was.

After dinner they stayed with him, conversing, until very late and then Longele said she was going. She wished Ngoso and Makole goodnight and she and Ndongo went out. Ndongo took the lantern which was in the parlour and opened the door.

'Sleep well,' Longele said to the girl on the verandah, holding an overturned basin over her head. She wore it like an enormous felt hat. She stepped into the rain.

'Yes, Aunty,' Ndongo said. 'You too sleep well. Tomorrow.'

She waited on the verandah until the woman had disappeared in the night. Then she sighed and went back to the house and shut the door; then, leaving the lamp on the table she went into Ngoso's room where another lamp was burning.

'It looks as though I too must go and sleep,' Makole said. 'I am very tired.'

'Wait,' Ndongo said, rising from the edge of Ngoso's bed. She slept in the same room, but on the floor where she spread a mat. 'Let me make the other room for you.'

After a moment or two Makole also got up.

'Tomorrow,' he said.

'Yes, tomorrow,' Ngoso barely managed to say.

24

To Ngoso it seemed a long time — even though it was only a matter of minutes — before Ndongo returned from the other room.

'Sit down,' he said.

'No,' she said. 'I have some cassavas to peel. I want to soak them tonight.'

'Can't they wait until tomorrow?' he asked, moaning. 'The cassavas, they can wait. They won't run, run away.'

'If I should wait until tomorrow I won't feel like peeling them any more. You don't know how lazy I get about those cassavas. They have been lying in the room for over a week now. Some are already going bad.'

She looked at him waiting for some sign from him that she might go. But no sign came and she sighed with feeling and turned towards the door; and hands behind her, she shuffled out of the room.

After a while he thought he heard voices. That headache! The fever.

And then a scandalous silence prevailed but for the humming sound of the rain. He wasn't hearing the voices any more. What were they doing? Were they together, knowing that he Ngoso was now a sick man and would find it difficult to leave that bed in order to surprise them in their intimacy?

His imagination reminded him of the pleasure and warmth women have in the depth of their thighs, real joy, the wonderful humidity, and he felt his thing getting up. He sighed, realizing for the first time with despair how much he loved women.

But he got over his passion when he began to feel suspicious to the point of restless jealousy. He tried hard and sat up. He pushed the blankets away from him and put his feet on the ground.

He rose from the bed and tied his loin-cloth firmly about him. And then a hot cloud rose about his head, a kind of giddiness and he reached for the nearest wall with both hands and leaned his head against it. He felt empty inside. He felt very weak. It was as if he was going to fall.

A feverish darkness rose at the back of his eyes and he felt himself weightless, drifting. And then for him nothing existed at that moment, not even his being for he ceased to feel himself. Life and death had no meaning, no essence. Everything was nothing, as they say, and everywhere was nowhere.

Then as if he had been cursed and condemned to experience life to the full, that is, to witness all its joy and participate in some of it, and see all its betrayals and a good deal of its suffering for many more years to come, the darkness in his eyes began to clear. He regained consciousness of the ground under him and the wall in front of him and the door on his left.

His knees felt very weak. But that didn't matter. He had to follow his imagination or be destroyed. He had to go and see for himself and react, drawing on what was left of his strength. So he dragged himself out of the room.

The parlour was in darkness. But there was light under the door of the room where he was convinced Ndongo and his friend Makole were struggling in the deep pleasure of tumultuous embraces.

But he soon discovered that he hadn't the strength to walk to that door. If he was to reach it he would either have to crawl on the ground or to support himself against the wall and advance like a blind man. He chose the wall and holding on to it he dragged himself along.

He got to the door. It easily gave way and he looked into

the room. The bed was empty. He went forward, feeling much stronger now. He took the lantern which was on a chair and looked under the bed. No one was there.

Had they chosen the kitchen then?

He replaced the lamp on the chair and shuffled painfully out of the room. Pleasure was turning everyone against him now that he was no longer a man of joy.

And his only brother was away at the fishing port! He was the only person he had on earth, the only one who would stand by him to the very end; and his step-aunt, of course.

He didn't hold on to the wall as he crossed the parlour towards the back door that led to the kitchen.

He opened the door and looked out.

The rain dropped like a waterfall from the eaves. Through the downpour he could see the reflection of the flames of the fireside dancing in the doorway of the kitchen.

The rain seemed to be increasing.

He felt like crying because of the rain and the cold and he was ill with a bad fever and he had become very weak.

He courageously stepped outside and was immediately drenched to the very insides of his thighs as he took the first few steps towards the kitchen. Then his knees weakened and as if pressed down by the rain he sank on the ground. And the rain and the winds were on him mercilessly.

The winds blew and blew and he thought they were warning him about something, reminding him of the past. There was no denying of his duty towards Njale's child. He had to live for that boy or that girl. But the winds were too hard on him and too rough.

Everything outside him was wind-swept. Nowhere could he find a last straw, except in himself — his sense of duty towards the child he loved even before its birth. Because of that child he had to rise and trudge towards life.

He willed himself to a standing position. He jogged forward. He was going to fall but he steadied himself. He took a few more steps and he was under the eaves of the kitchen.

He clung to a post and moaning he managed to get under the shelter of the verandah.

He listened. But he only heard the voice of the rain, howling, cursing. And the whining of the winds.

Leaning against the wall he moved forward. But he was soon feeling so exhausted that he had to stop in order to regain his breath. He closed his eyes, his head against the wall.

When he felt better, he opened his eyes, took a few more steps and then leaning forward, gripping the door-frame with both hands, he looked into the kitchen.

Ndongo was on a low stool, a cassava in her hand; she was peeling it. A basin was on her left. The cassavas she had peeled were in it; and on her right was a basket of cassavas still to be peeled.

She sensed the presence of someone and when she looked up and saw that it was Ngoso, she dropped the cassava and knife.

'A ghost!' she cried, covering her face with both hands and trembling because she thought he had died and it was his ghost which had come to say good-bye to her. '*Bińo ya e!*' she cried. '*Bińo ya e!* Help, help! A ghost!'

'Ndongo,' Ngoso gasped, 'Ndongo,' he added, shivering, 'Ndongo, it's me. It's not a ghost. I'm not dead. Where is Makole?'

She took off her hands from her face and seeing how drenched he was alarm took the place of horror on her face.

She hurried towards him.

'What happened?' she asked, trembling. 'Why did you leave the room?'

'I say where is Makole?'

'Isn't he in the room?'

162

'He's not there,' he said. 'Where is he?'

'Maybe he went out.'

'To do what under this rain? Has he a woman here?'

'Yes.'

'Who?'

She lowered her look.

'I say who?' he repeated. 'Aunty Longele?'

'I don't know,' she said, still not looking at him.

He turned round, telling himself that now no one had the right to persuade him not to go to his farm to drive that Bakweriman.

Ndongo took his hand. They walked in the rain towards the main hut.

It was true that he hadn't made any direct pass at the woman. It would have been improper. That was why he hadn't done it. And so his desire for her had grown through the years into desperate affection. She seemed to like it and had encouraged his feelings. But all was now over. She had become just another woman.

Ndongo didn't mind that she was getting wet. She knew how he was feeling about Longele.

When they got to the parlour she went to his room and brought the lantern and a towel. She put the lantern on the table and gave him the towel after she had made him take off his wet loin-cloth.

He wiped himself like a man in a dream, feeling his heart shedding all the love it had had for his step-aunt.

Ndongo went into the room and brought a blanket.

'Wrap it round you,' she said.

There was pity in her eyes and he was ashamed of himself.

Shivering, he wrapped the blanket round him and sat down.

'I'll warm some water for you,' she said. 'You must wash before going back to the bed.' She sighed and shook her head. 'I don't know why you did that.'

He didn't say anything. So much of him was now in the past. But he was left with one obsessive dream — that of his children of tomorrow.

Staring in front of him, he sighed like an old man, seeing his farm in the rainy season.

25

The train from N'kongsamba rumbled from station to station: suku-suku-suku-suku-suku-suku-suku-suku-suku-suku-suku-suku-suku-suku-suku-suku-suku-suku-suku-suku-suku-suku-suku-suku-suku-suku, with the illusion of racing forests, palm trees and telegraph poles, suku-suku-suku-suku-suku-suku-suku-suku-ho-ho-o-o-ho!

From time to time the wind bore a spark into a coach and burnt a hole into someone's dress. The smell of burning cotton, silk or wool and people slapped themselves on the shoulders, on the back, fearing that it was their dresses which were burning.

And Ewudu was there, seeing the life-size image of Ngoso in her imagination, suku-suku-suku-suku-suku-suku-suku-suku, she had gone to N'kongsamba hoping that she would feel better there; one week came and passed; then another week; nothing happened to her memories of him, suku-suku-suku-suku-suku-suku-suku-suku, she continued to refuse men as she had been doing since her arrival in Duala from his farm five weeks ago.

And it was over a week now since she had been expecting that blood and by now she was sure it wouldn't come until after nine months. That was what had given her the courage to return. Njale no longer had any advantage over her. And she knew what children meant to him, suku-suku-suku-suku-suku-suku-suku-suku; the blood would come in nine months' time; and that would be with a new life. She saw the child!

No one on that train could have imagined how happy she was, sitting there, so thoughtful, looking out of the window at the forest and the telegraph poles.

When the train pulled into Bomono Station and stopped, those passengers, mostly local folk, who were to come down there did so.

Like the others, Ewudu managed to get down just in time as the Station Master soon blew his whistle:

Pirrrrrrrrrrrrrr!

And the train pulled out of the station: suk, suk, suk, suk, suk, suk, suk, suku-suku-suku-suku-suku-suku. . . .

Most of the passengers who came down were Pongowomen. They were dynamic and noisy and they wore gay print dresses. Here and there along the rails outside the station they were lifting their basins to their heads. The basins contained their belongings. Some of the women held long sugar-canes.

For the season it was a very sunny day; and Ewudu told herself that she was lucky.

Her travelling bag in her hand she joined the crowd which was converging on the exit where a controller took their tickets which had been perforated on the train.

Once out of the station she turned right, crossed the rails and followed the motor-road from N'kongsamba.

She walked as fast as she could. But she hadn't long steps because she was small.

A palm-tree plantation was on her right. On her left, the bush. She heard the sound of a lorry. She went further to her right to keep out of the way. And there was the lorry, covered with red mud, rushing at top speed towards Bonaberi and Duala. An apprentice driver was perched on its roof.

Zuoh-ng!

Terrific speed and yet it was so loaded. It rounded the bend in the distance and was gone, leaving behind it a cloud of dust.

After the motor-road she followed a bush-path which ran along the palm-tree plantation. It wasn't altogether a bush-path as lorries which collected palm-nuts used it from time to time. Their wheels had left tracks on the grass.

Then she left the plantation behind. She passed one village; then another. At this hour of the day people were still away, working on their farms and so the tiny villages looked very empty. Once she saw a goat and then hens and chicks and in the second village an old woman going into her hut.

She entered the forest on the other side of which Ngoso's farm was.

Tall trees with very huge trunks. Some of their roots rose above the ground, strong, humped. Birds called, others answered, sounding forlorn and happy in turns.

The branches shook, far-away, above her, as if near the sky. The breezy flapping of the wings of great birds. Fruits dropped.

She descended a steep hill. Swampy stretches were ahead. Insects chirped in the half-darkness of the forest.

At the foot of the hill she picked up a stave from the roadside. Quite a number of people had crossed the swamps that afternoon and others earlier on in the morning; or maybe the previous day because there were many staves on the roadside. They had been left there so that other people might use them while wading through the mud.

Ewudu stepped on a log which had been thrown across the

166

stream at the foot of the hill. It served as a bridge.

After the stream she waded through the mud. Then she walked, very carefully, on another log. She just had to slip and she would have found herself on the mud, her bag a yard or so away and soiled.

The way seemed long, very long, and it was very slippery and muddy. Some of the logs were submerged in the water and the mud. You had to feel with your stave to find where the logs were; and that was what she did and she found it all very tedious.

The way wasn't in reality so far; but because one advanced gradually it seemed very far indeed.

She climed a hill and walked and walked and then she got to another stretch of swamp land. After crossing it she felt like resting. But she decided against it. If I should sit down now, she thought, it will be very difficult for me to get up again. After all I'm no longer that far from his home.

She walked and walked.

The sky appeared before her. She had left the forest behind. She was now in Ngonjo.

She walked between cassava farms and passed by the corner of a hut. She could hear people conversing inside.

She passed, descended a hill and that was the river — wide, silent, constant. It was now very peaceful.

Ngoso! And something scattered in her heart, something sweet like mangoes falling from a wind-battered mango tree.

She walked faster, along the river.

Anxiety. She had been feeling it all along. But now it was acute. She feared he might not want her back. No, he would want her back, she reassured herself and walked even faster.

Then it occurred to her that Mudeka Market was the following day. Had he put plantains in his canoe and gone to the market?

No, she told herself. It is still too early. The sun hasn't even

167

set. If at all he intends going to the market it will be later tonight.
But supposing he isn't at home?

She hurried on. Sometimes the path got quite near the river and
she saw the water through the reeds.

26

And this was his farm!

She slowed down her pace. Her heart was beating as it had
never beaten before. She walked into his compound and then her
heart sank.

A padlock was on the door. She put down her bag and went to
look down the beach. His canoe was there. She went back to the
verandah and sat down on the ground and waited until the sun
began to go down and she felt very sleepy because she hadn't
been able to sleep during the night, thinking of him.

She rose, took her bag and went round the hut and opened the
kitchen door and went in. A log was burning in the fireside. She
pushed the door shut, sat down, and leaning against the wall
behind her, prepared to go to sleep.

She was very tired. Once more she wondered why he couldn't
go and live in Mongo and come from there to work on the farm.
Certainly there were months during which he had very little
work to do; so why live here every day of the year?

Having come back with his child in her she began to see herself living on the farm all her life and she felt the profound melancholy of such an existence; for although the men and women paddling on the river often sang of love and of hope and although there was real happiness and warm family life on some of the farms, what predominated was sadness, the transition from one age to another.

Old Dikodu and others of his age told stories of the time when the riverbanks had been densely populated. Farm houses had been everywhere along the river and Mongo had been Mongo: wrestling matches, masquerades and dances; and their long race canoe manned by some eighty sturdy men in white loin-cloths won canoe-races in the sea in Duala!

Life on the river had been very lively, almost like town life. And whenever Dikodu talked of those days there was nostalgia in his eyes and in his voice.

Even Ngoso had talked to Ewudu about how there had been more people on the farms when he was a little boy. He told her what his father had told him and it was like the stories Dikodu told about the river.

But now none of that general boisterousness remained. Farm huts were far apart for most of the farms had been abondoned. The few that remained, like Ngoso's, were lonely survivals of the past. In each of them a farmer lived with his wife and their children if they had any. And if they hadn't, or they were away in the city, they lived in their hut, the two of them, yesterday, today and during the days to come until one of them died.

As you paddled on the river you saw such lonely settlements. A hut sheltering a woman, a widow, or a man, a widower, with the only sign of life, should the man or the woman be working in the hut or at the back of the farm, being the canoe down the beach and the hens and cocks on the edge of the compound. Or you saw them at times under the cocoa trees. And when you didn't see them you heard the crowing of the cocks. Then there was also the smoke spiralling skywards — another sign that the farm was still inhabited.

Sometimes, however, you saw a hut and thought it was inhabited when in fact it wasn't. Its owner might have abondoned it or he or she might have died. And after weeks, or months, grass climbed on the walls of the hut, then on the roof and finally pulled it down.

Many months later, people paddling on the river pointed at what had once been a well-tended farm and they said *semekakale*, that is, such and such a man or woman, had lived there; and those who knew talked about his or her family.

They talked about how the man had been; how he had died. And if he had left a widow, they talked about the woman. How she had been and how she had followed her husband, that is, how she too had died.

Feeling very weary, Ewudu closed her eyes and went to sleep.

2 7

When she woke up in the night she thought she heard someone in the main hut.

'*A*-Ngoso,' she called, getting up and taking her bag.

She went out of the kitchen and to the back door of the main hut. There was light inside and she heard footsteps coming towards her.

'*A*-Ngoso,' she said. 'But why aren't you answering?'

Then she thought that maybe it was Njale.

The door was opened and someone held up a lantern.

'*A*-Mbongo!' Ewudu said.

'How?' Ngoso's brother said. 'Have you come?'

'Yes.'

'Come in.'

She went in and he shut the door.

'Where are the others?' she asked, putting down her bag.

'Njale has gone back to her people.'

'And Ngoso?'

'Follow me,' he said, going out, the lantern in his hand.

He led the way under the cocoa trees until he got to the little burial ground where he raised the lantern at a fresh mound of earth.

'Dead?' she cried, throwing herself on the ground.

'Yes,' he replied. 'Dead.'

'*Aye-e*!'

She wept throughout most of that night; and unable to fall asleep and feeling very sad, Mbongo went out.

The sky was very dark and a light rain was falling making eerie sounds under the cocoa trees.

He too began to cry.

'*A*-Ngoso,' he sobbed desparately when he got to the burial ground. '*A*-Ngoso, Ewudu has come.' He did not weep aloud; and only sobbed and sobbed, his mouth wide open. 'Ewudu has come; Ewudu has come. She's in the house, *a*-Ngoso. She's crying . . .' He was mourning his brother and mourning himself in advance for he knew that one day, which could be tomorrow, he too would be lying under a cold mound of earth like one of those which were before him in the darkness. 'Ngoso, you get up then,' he sobbed. 'Please, please, Ngoso! So you mean we shall never see you again? Never? Oh, Ngoso, *a*-Ngoso. . . .'

He turned round and still weeping walked back slowly to the hut.

But he didn't go in. He stood on the verandah for a long time, staring at the wet night.

Down the river the second floods were subsiding.

Mbongo sighed and went in. Ewudu was sitting on the floor and staring in front of her.

28

It was in the morning that he talked to her of Ngoso's illness and of his death.

'But why did he refuse the medicine?' Ewudu asked him, her headscarf tied like a belt round her waist.

'I don't know,' Mbongo said. 'Longele said she was surprised. He wouldn't even look at her and wouldn't let her touch him. He was going and he was going.'

'*Uweh*!' Ewudu sighed.

'Makole says they tried to dissuade him. They tried. They said everything; and a little rain was outside, mind you. But he refused to listen to them. Shivering, he took his bag and paddle and went to the beach and Longele and Ndongo locked their doors and followed him and Makole.

'He climbed into his canoe and Makole asked him not to

bother himself, that he would go up with him and he would do the paddling. Longele and Ndongo went back to the town and returned with paddles and followed them in Makole's canoe.

'They say by the time they got here he was so ill that all he could say when he saw Ekema was to ask him to leave his house at once.

'They say Ekema looked at him, shook his head and lowered his eyes. When he looked up again he promised to leave. He took Makole outside and asked him if he couldn't stay in his house for a few days? He said he couldn't go while Ngoso was so ill. He would have no peace of mind. Couldn't he stay in Makole's place for a few days? He would go as soon as Ngoso began to get well.

'Makole agreed.

'Ngoso died the following night,' Mbongo went on, 'almost the same time as I arrived in Mongo from the fishing port and was told that they had gone up with him to the farm. I left Mongo immediately, not knowing that he was already dead.'

'Ngoso,' Ewudu breathed, beginning to sob again, 'Ngoso—'

'Many people came to the funeral — people from Mongo, Mudeka, Benge, Duala. Many people.'

'Did Jengu come?'

'Yes, she and Esadi.'

'Ekema, Ekema, was he at the funeral?'

'Yes,' Mbongo said. 'He only left the following day. I think he regretted very much what he did. He even offered me some money to help me with the expenses. I told him to keep his money. But I don't think he's a bad man. He has a clean heart.'

29

News of Ewudu's return reached Ekema after a few days and on the eve of the following Mudeka Market he was on the farm.

He met Mbongo sitting on the verandah.

Ekema was in a large loin-cloth over which he wore a brown shirt. A felt hat was on his head, a packet of cigarettes in the breast pocket of his shirt. He was barefooted.

'*Uweh*!' Mbongo exclaimed. 'We have a visitor.'

They exchanged greetings and shook hands.

He offered him a seat and Ekema sat down.

'Ewudu,' he called.

'*E?*' she answered from the backyard. '*Ná ye?*'

'*E,*' he said. 'Your man has come.'

'Who?'

'You just come and see.'

'When did she arrive?' Ekema asked.

'Four days ago.'

'From Duala?'

'No,' Mbongo said just as Ewudu came to the verandah.

Her face was calm. Her eyes betrayed no particular emotion as they met Ekema's.

'Won't you shake my hand?' he asked her.

She looked at Mbongo.

'Shake his hand,' Mbongo said.

They shook hands.

'How are you?' he asked.

'I am well.'

'Mother said I should greet you.'

'Is she well?' Ewudu asked coldly.

'Yes,' Ekema said.

But when his mother had asked him to greet Ewudu there had been a strong hint of sarcasm in her voice which, however, Ekema chose to ignore.

Ewudu went back to the kitchen.

There was a little palmwine in the house. Mbongo brought it to the verandah and went in for cups.

They were drinking when Ekema said he didn't know if Mbongo knew why he had come.

'You came to take Ewudu,' Mbongo said.

'Yes,' Ekema said, looking into his cup.

Yes, Mbongo thought. Take her to wherever you like. Who knows whether or not the dead see? With his jealousy Ngoso may not like her living with me. Take her away.

'But I can't settle that matter alone,' he told Ekema. 'Wait later when Makole will sit down with two or three other people. Then we shall discuss. Don't worry.'

30

The two men ate the afternoon meal together and then they went to Makole's place. They met him making preparations for the market. Mbongo called him aside and told him the purpose of

175

Ekema's journey. He said later that evening Makole should come to his farm so that they might discuss the matter. Makole said he would come.

Then Mbongo and Ekema went to Missaka where Mbongo bought a demijohn of palmwine and invited a number of people among whom were Malende, the palmwine tapper and Dikodu, the story-teller.

They all came to the farm later that evening; and drinking the palmwine, they conversed. Ewudu sat alone in the kitchen.

Makole looked at Mbongo.

'Ewudu,' Mbongo called.

She didn't answer but she came. No one asked her to sit down.

'Ekema,' Mbongo said, 'so tell us what brought you.'

'I came to take her,' he said boldly.

All eyes were turned towards her; save Ekema's.

'You are looking at me,' Mbongo said to Ewudu. 'You heard what he said.'

'You want me to go?'

'Isn't he your man?' Mbongo said; and then, looking at the others, he said: 'Or has someone else something to say?'

'What else is there to say?' Malende said.

'We didn't buy her,' Dikodu said, 'She's free to go if she says she's going.'

Ewudu turned away and went out to the back yard. She burst into tears.

'But I'm pregnant,' she wept. 'I am pregnant.'

The people in the parlour exchanged glances.

'What?' Ekema shouted. 'You are pregnant?'

Ewudu went on crying and didn't reply.

Mbongo stood up; and turning towards the door that led to the backyard, he asked:

'Whose child?'

But Ewudu only went on crying.

'I say whose child?' Mbongo shouted.

'Your brother's,' she wept, 'It's Ngoso's child.'

Mbongo sat down. He looked at the disillusioned Ekema who had been looking so hopeful and proud only a while ago. He found himself pitying him for like Ekema, Mbongo too had a clean heart.

Ekema looked up.

'Ewudu, come here!' he shouted desperately.

She continued to cry.

'Ewudu,' Mbongo called. 'Ewudu, come here.'

Because he was the brother of her child's father, she obeyed and came to the parlour.

'What you've just said is it true?' Ekema asked her.

'Yes,' she sobbed, nodding.

'Will you still take her?' Malende asked.

Ekema was angry. He was disappointed. But he couldn't understand why he still felt he had to go away with her.

'Yes,' he said to Malende.

'She says she's pregnant,' Mbongo said.

'I know,' Ekema said, his eyes on Ewudu.

'You still want her?' Dikodu asked.

'Yes,' Ekema said even though he knew that if he married her as he meant to do he would be uneasy all his life.

He was already suffering the suffering of those who continue to love even after they had been betrayed.

Suddenly Mbongo didn't want Ewudu to go anymore.

'Will you go with him?' he asked her.

'If you say I should go,' she sobbed, 'if you say I should go.'

That was not what he had expected she would say.

'Yes,' he said; and then he remembered what Etaka had said Ngoso had said to her in Mongo when she had asked him to go and bring Njale back. Ours is ours. That was what he had said, meaning their child would always be theirs whether or not its

177

mother ran away with it. 'Makole is going down tomorrow,' Mbongo said, almost reluctantly. 'You'll go down with him.'

'Yes,' Makole said, looking at Ewudu and then at Ekema.

31

That night Mbongo dreamt of Ngoso.

When he woke up in the morning he couldn't remember what his brother had told him. He was worried because of this and was very sad as Makole was paddling out of the beach with Ewudu and Ekema in the canoe.

He stood there, alone, and watched the canoe become smaller and smaller in the distance until Makole who was at the helm seemed to be sitting on the water, paddling towards the south which was covered with clouds.

I hope it doesn't rain on them, Mbongo thought. An ibis was on the opposite bank, pacing the mud left behind by the flood.

He began to think of his late brother again and tears came into his eyes as he turned round and went back to the hut.